burnt orange

color me wasted

melody carlson

Th1nk Books
an imprint of NavPress®

www.navpress.com

TH1NK Books is an imprint of NavPress. TH1NK is a registered trademark of NavPress. Absence of ® in connection with marks of NavPress or other parties does not indicate an absence of registration of those marks.

ISBN 1-57683-533-2

Cover design by studiogearbox.com
Cover photo by Powerstock/Superstock
Creative Team: Gabe Filkey, Arvid Wallen, Erin Healy, Cara Iverson, Laura Spray, Pat Miller

Published in association with the literary agency of Sara A. Fortenberry.

Carlson, Melody.
Burnt orange : color me wasted / Melody Carlson.
p. cm. -- (Truecolors series ; 5)
Summary: The daughter of a pastor justifies going to drinking parties as helping others, disregarding the feelings of real friends.
ISBN 1-57683-533-2
[1. Alcohol--Fiction. 2. Traffic accidents--Fiction. 3. High schools--Fiction. 4. Schools--Fiction. 5. Christian life--Fiction.] I. Title.
PZ7.C216637Bu 2005
[Fic]--dc22

2004022364

Printed in Canada

1 2 3 4 5 6 7 8 9 10 / 09 08 07 06 05

Other Books by Melody Carlson

Pitch Black (NavPress)
Torch Red (NavPress)
Deep Green (NavPress)
Dark Blue (NavPress)
Diary of a Teenage Girl series (Multnomah)
Degrees of Guilt series (Tyndale)
Crystal Lies (WaterBrook)
Finding Alice (WaterBrook)
Looking for Cassandra Jane (Tyndale)

one

"Hello, my name is Amber Conrad," I say in my most serious voice, "and I'm an alcoholic." I'm standing at the podium at the front of the room wearing a new T-shirt and a deadpan expression. I take a deep breath and continue. "And I am here tonight to admit that I am in need of serious help."

Suddenly my friends burst out laughing and, of course, I can't help but laugh too. I step away from the wooden podium and head over to the kitchen area to help Simi and Lisa set up. It's actually youth-group night at our church, and the three of us got here early because we're in charge of setting up snacks.

"You happy now that I fessed up?" I ask Simi Gartolini in my most sarcastic voice. Simi can take it. My best friend since middle school, she's been on my case all day long about this.

"Hey, I *never* accused you of being an alcoholic," she responds in a slightly defensive tone as she fills a bowl with cheese twists. "I only said I was concerned that you went to that party last night."

"Yeah," says Lisa Chan as she arranges soft-drink cans into a cooler full of ice. "What's up with that, Amber? You knew what those kids were up to. Everyone knows they're just a bunch of alkies."

I laugh at this absurdity. "Yeah, sure, Lisa. Everyone at that party is an alcoholic. Get real."

"Well, they're boozers," she retorts in that slightly superior tone. "You can't deny that."

"I think you guys are just jealous," I say, hoping I can change the subject from drinking to something a little more comfortable. "I think you're picking on me just because you two didn't get an invite to Tommy Campbell's party."

"Tommy Campbell's a snob and a moron." Simi makes a face as she pops a bright orange cheese twist into her mouth. "I don't even know why you think he's so cool anyway."

"Oooh," I say to Simi now. "Sounding pretty judgmental for a Christian, don't ya think?" Then I grab a bag of tortilla chips and attempt to open it, finally resorting to using my teeth to rip the stubborn plastic bag.

"I'm not judging. I just think God expects us to have some common sense when it comes to choosing friends," she says, "and I think your dad does too."

"Yeah," adds Lisa. "Going to that party was a dumb move, Amber. I mean, kids look up to us as Christians and we're supposed to be the leaders in youth group. Seriously, what's going to happen when word gets around that Amber Conrad, daughter of Pastor Conrad, is a beer-drinking party girl now?"

"Man, I never should've told you guys about it." I sigh loudly and roll my eyes. "Besides, like I already told you, I only had one beer and I didn't even drink the whole thing. Seriously, it's no big deal, okay? The only reason I was there at all was just so I could witness to Claire Phillips—"

"Yeah, you bet," says Simi. "That's a great idea, Amber—go to a drinking party, have a beer, and then witness to someone."

Lisa laughs. "Yeah, brilliant plan. Maybe you should share your strategy with the youth group tonight. Maybe we could take it to the bars."

Okay, now I'm feeling pretty defensive. I mean, what right do these two have to judge me and everyone else on the planet for that matter? Like, who died and made these two girls God?

"Whatever," I finally say as if I don't really care. "Think what you want about me." I use a slightly wounded tone, hoping to garner some pity, but then I hear the sound of voices coming down the hallway toward us and I know it's too late. "But hey," I say quickly, "it's not like you have to tell everybody in youth group about my sinful ways."

"You don't think they'll hear about it anyway?" asks Simi.

"I don't see how." Then I get more serious. "Come on, you guys," I plead, "don't make this into a big deal, okay? I mean, I trusted you with this. I thought you were my friends."

Simi smiles now. "Okay, Amber. My lips are sealed."

"Yeah, mine too," says Lisa, although she looks slightly smug. "You happy now?"

I shrug. "Hey, I appreciate it."

"But you can't blame us if the story leaks out anyway."

I know she's probably right. It's not like I can really keep a lid on the big news that I, Amber Conrad, a slightly nerdish pastor's kid, went to Tommy's party last night. I know as well as anyone how rumors can fly through the information mill at South Ashton, but usually the rumors are about someone else. I don't think there's ever been a rumor about me personally. Like, who would care? Of course, now that I'm a senior and graduation is only two months away, well, maybe I don't really care either. I mean, hey, maybe it's about time I did something worth talking about!

But as the room starts filling up with youth-group kids, I'm not so sure anymore. I mean, do I really want these guys to know what I was up to last night? These are church kids I have known for years—kids whose parents are close friends with my parents—and, for the most part, they're fairly nice kids. Now, I know that everyone has their problems and stuff and nobody's perfect, but these are the kinds of kids who really try to follow God and live their lives for his glory. And for the most part, they are my friends too. But the truth is, I'm actually thinking they're just a little bit boring right now. Maybe I think this more tonight than usual. Of course, I don't let this show. I know better than that.

Instead, I smile and say "hey" to everyone, just like always. I even compliment Tyler Addison on his haircut, although I honestly think it's way too short for his long and narrow head. In fact, he kind of looks like Homer Simpson right now. And I ask Laney Edwards if she's lost weight, and this makes her smile. The truth is, she looks heavier than ever, and that fuzzy hot-pink sweater isn't helping one bit.

Okay, I'll admit it: I'm a total hypocrite sometimes. But it's like I'm supposed to have this happy outlook on life all the time, like I'm supposed to make everyone feel good about themselves even if I'm telling a big fat lie. It's just how a pastor's family is supposed to act, you know?

Oh sure, my parents never actually say as much. In fact, I'm pretty sure my dad would deny he acts like that at all, which in my opinion is just another form of deceit. Okay, in defense of my well-meaning parents, I think maybe they actually sort of believe the outrageous things they say. It's like they've been doing it for so long that they can't even tell the difference between the truth and phony baloney.

Anyway, I've studied them over the years, and I've learned from them as they play their little feel-good game without ever thinking twice. They just smile and tell their little white lies and act like it's no big deal. And naturally, being a good daughter, I just follow their lead and do the same.

That's probably what had gotten Claire Phillips' attention last week. It looked like she was having a bad day, so I complimented her on her outfit, which, although I suspect by the labels was probably expensive, didn't really look that great on her. It actually made her look stockier than she is. Not that she's exactly chubby, but she's kind of short and compact—that curvy kind of compact that guys seem to appreciate, including her boyfriend, Tommy Campbell.

"Thanks, Amber," she said to me with a bright smile. Then she asked if I had my notes from English lit on me.

"Sure," I told her. "Do you want to borrow them? I noticed you missed class yesterday."

"Yeah, I was sick," she said. "But I don't want to get behind. Mr. Sorenson is hard enough on us as it is."

"Man, I know," I agreed. "He gave me a C for midterms."

"You got a C?" Her eyes grew wide.

"Yeah, and when I asked him why, he said it was to push me harder for the final grade. Can you believe it? I've really been trying to keep my GPA up."

"Man, that's harsh," she said as I handed her my notes. "I'll get these back to you in time for class," she promised.

I should know better than to loan out my notes, but for some reason, I trusted Claire—and all right, she's one of the most popular girls in our class and I wouldn't mind if she liked me better. So I was pleasantly surprised when she returned my notes, in perfect condition I might add, and then actually invited me to come to Tommy's party.

"I can invite whoever I want," she assured me as we walked into Mr. Sorenson's class. "So, I hope you'll come, Amber. I'd really like to see you there." Then she laughed. "And everyone knows Tommy's parties are the best."

I blinked and tried not to look too surprised, and then I told her I'd think about it. By the end of class, she'd already written down his address and phone number on a torn-off corner of notebook paper. "Here," she said. "Now, seriously, I want you to come, okay?"

"Okay," I said and then added, "I mean, I'll think about it."

"Good." She smiled. "Since there are only two months until graduation, I've been trying to get to know more kids, you know, so I'll know more people at our class reunions."

Now, I had to laugh at that. "I guess I haven't been thinking that far ahead," I admitted.

She grinned. "Well, maybe you should."

And that's how I ended up going to Tommy Campbell's party. And here's the truth: I actually had fun. And it wasn't boring at all. Claire was really nice to me, and then her other friends were fairly nice too. It's like everyone just really cut loose and had a great time. Sure, some kids drank too much and one girl even got sick and threw up in the pool, which really put a damper on swimming. But I didn't get drunk and I didn't get sick. Mostly, I just had an unexpectedly fun time. And, really, what's wrong with that? I mean, even Jesus drank wine with his friends. And wasn't his first miracle turning water into wine? So, seriously, what's the problem?

two

To my relief, no one in youth group seems to know about my previous evening's activities. So, I sit in the back with Simi and listen as Glen Stanley (our youth pastor) tells a funny story about how his new Doberman puppy is systematically destroying everything in his studio apartment. Then suddenly my cell phone rings and everyone turns around and glares at me. I feel sort of silly, since my own dad always makes a big deal of reminding the congregation to turn off their phones during church services.

I can't imagine who'd be calling me now, since most of my friends are right here in the youth house. But I wave my hand in a kind of apology as I rush out to the hallway to answer the call. I hope nothing's wrong at home.

"Hello?"

"Hey, Amber," says an unfamiliar girl's voice. "What's up?"

"Who is this?"

"It's Claire." She laughs. "Don't you remember me, girlfriend?"

"Oh." I try not to sound surprised. "Yeah, sure. I just didn't recognize your voice and the connection isn't that clear."

"Oh, I'll speak up. *Can you hear me now?*"

I laugh at this tired joke as I go through the kitchen and out the back door, where I can talk without being overheard by the youth group. "Yeah, yeah. I can hear you now."

"Well, I was just stuck at home and thought I'd give you a call and see if you want to do something."

I consider telling her that I'm busy tonight, but instead I stupidly ask, "What did you have in mind?"

"Oh, I just thought maybe we could hang together. You have a car, don't you?"

"Yeah . . ."

"Well, want to come over here and pick me up and we can find something exciting to do?" She laughs. "Or at least something more entertaining than watching this stupid rerun of *The O.C.*"

I'm surprised Claire is stuck at home on a Saturday night. I'd always assumed that someone like her would be hanging with her friends or out on a date with Tommy—anything more interesting than sitting at home or being at youth group.

For whatever unexplainable reason, I agree to go pick Claire up. But now this means I have to blow off Simi and ask her to get a ride home with someone else. I'm guessing Lisa will cover for me.

"Is something wrong?" Simi asks after I tell her that I have to leave.

"I just need to get home," I say. And I feel a real stab of guilt and wonder, *Why am I lying to Simi?* It's not like it's a big deal to go do something with Claire. Even so, I feel certain that Simi wouldn't understand. How could she when *I* don't?

She nods. "Well, call me later."

I promise to do that and then take off jogging to my car that's parked in front of the youth house. But as I go, I feel guilty about ditching Simi. I remember the promise I made to her when her parents moved to the other side of town last year and she was all worried that the distance would affect our friendship. "Don't worry,"

I told her. "We've been best friends for like five years now. Nothing's going to change that." And so she got permission to finish her senior year at South Ashton instead of going to North Ashton (a school we pretend to hate). The only problem was that it became pretty inconvenient to share rides since it like doubles the driving time. The only reason I gave her a ride to church tonight was because we were already hanging together anyway, so really she should understand this whole thing.

As guilty as I feel, I also have this very real sense of excitement and adventure, almost like I'm playing hooky or something—not that I've ever done that before. But something about skipping out on youth group to go hang with someone as cool as Claire seems rather risky and thrilling.

I unlock my Neon and climb in and then glance nervously around the interior to observe that it's relatively neat in here tonight. I usually let my car get pretty junky during the school week, you know, with fast-food bags and wrappers and stuff from school and, well, whatever. But then I usually give it a cleanout on weekends. Otherwise, my dad peeks in and makes some stupid comment like, "Maybe you'll want to be a garbage-truck driver someday, Amber." Fortunately, I did the cleanout this morning.

I follow the directions Claire gave me and drive toward a new development that's not too far from where I live—well, in earth miles anyway. River's Edge is an expensive subdivision that's situated around an eighteen-hole golf course, and I've heard that the houses there run about a half million apiece.

I didn't realize that Claire was so rich, but I have to admit that I'm curious to see where she lives. I mean, I was pretty impressed with Tommy's house last night. The fact that it had a huge inground pool was pretty impressive, but that seems to be nothing compared to the houses I'm driving past now.

I finally locate her home and after parking my suddenly cheap-looking Neon in the wide brick driveway, I walk toward the front door, feeling like an intruder. Not only that, but I begin to wonder if this isn't just some kind of trick. I mean, why would someone like Claire invite me over here on a Saturday night?

"Hey, you!" calls out Claire as she opens the big double doors. "Come on in."

"Cool house," I tell her as I walk into a huge foyer with a marble floor that looks like it might've come straight from Italy.

She just shrugs. "I liked our old house in The Willows a lot better. It had more personality. But my stepdad thinks this one is more impressive. Whatever."

I glance past the foyer to where a spacious living room with white furnishings looks out over what I'm assuming is the golf course. It looks like something out of a movie set.

"Who's here?" calls a female voice from somewhere in the house.

"It's my friend Amber," yells Claire as she picks up her purse. "We're going out."

But before we get out the front door, a tall, pretty blonde woman appears. "Do you want to introduce me to your friend?"

Claire pauses and then forces a smile. "Yeah, this is Amber Conrad, Mom. She's a friend from school."

Her mom seems to study me carefully, and I wonder if I measure up. "I don't think I've seen you before," she finally says. "You go to school with Claire?"

I nod. "Yeah, I'm a senior too."

She looks back at Claire. "And what are you two doing this evening?"

"Just hanging." Then Claire rolls her eyes. "If it makes you feel any better, Amber's dad is the pastor of Grace Fellowship and Amber is a *nice* girl." She looks at me as though this should make some kind of sense, which it does not.

But this information seems to reassure her mother, who is suddenly smiling. "Oh, well, that's good. You girls have fun, then. But don't forget your curfew, Claire."

Then we are outside and Claire is muttering something I can't quite make out. "Moms," she finally says.

"Yeah, what was up with that?" I ask as I get into my car.

"It's a long story." She sighs loudly as she leans back into the passenger seat. "Let's just say that my mom doesn't trust me right now."

"Why?" I ask as I pull out of the driveway.

"I got my driver's license suspended a couple of weeks ago."

"What for?"

"I got a dewey."

"Huh?"

"You know, a ticket for driving under the influence."

"Oh." I make a face. "Bummer."

"You're telling me. Anyway, my mom's been freaked ever since that happened. It's like paranoia has set in and she thinks everyone is a bad influence on me. I mean, seriously, I was grounded for two weeks. I'm barely out now."

I nod and suddenly begin to understand why Claire might be so interested in my friendship lately. Maybe I'm "safe." Well, whatever. And, who knows, maybe I will be a good influence on her. Maybe I wasn't too far off in my claim to want to witness to her.

"Why don't you drive over to Brookstone," she suggests as I exit her development. She's pulling out her cell phone and calling someone.

"Haley," she says in a happy voice. "Where is everyone tonight?" She pauses and says a couple of "uh-huhs" and then hangs up and turns to me. "Just as I thought."

"What's that?"

"They're all at Kent Fischer's house. His parents are gone this weekend."

"Another party?" I ask, suddenly feeling a little uneasy—not only about the idea of what might possibly be another drinking party but also about the names of the kids just mentioned. Kent and Haley are both just as popular as Claire, and while the idea of spending time with these kids sounds intriguing, it's also a little unnerving. Plus, I would've put on a better outfit had I known.

She shakes her head. "No, this isn't a party as much as a casual social gathering. You know, just friends hanging together."

"But I'm not exactly in that group," I begin.

She laughs. "Don't worry about that. You're with *me*."

I grip the steering wheel more tightly. *Okay,* I'm telling myself, *just relax—this could be fun.* Even so, I'm a bundle of nerves by the time we walk in the door of Kent's house. But I try to act like it's no big deal, like I actually fit in with these kids, like I'm not aware of the possibility that Claire might simply be using me—partly for a ride and partly to play the "good girl" to convince her mom that she's found the straight and narrow. But here's what's weird. I'm not sure that I care. It's like I want to try this to see if somehow, someway, I might actually be able to fit in. I don't even know why. I mean, I think it's actually sort of shallow and stupid, but at the same time it's like I can't help myself.

"Want a beer?" asks Slater Ross, a guy who probably doesn't even know my name.

I kind of shrug, unsure of what to do. "I don't really like the taste of beer," I finally say.

He nods. "Yeah, I know what you mean." Then he grins. "I'll go find something you'll like."

I try not to look too interested as I watch him heading for the kitchen. Slater is tall and extremely good-looking. He reminds me of a young Tom Cruise. He's also really good at track and cross-country. To be honest, I don't expect him to return.

I try not to look too surprised when he does return. He holds out a tumbler of what appears to be orange juice. "Try this," he says with a handsome smile.

"What is it?" I ask as I skeptically peer at the glass.

"A screwdriver."

Well, I'm sure my expression gives away my ignorance, but he just laughs. "It's a drink, silly—just vodka and orange juice. But it tastes way better than beer." He hands it to me. "Just give it a try."

Well, I know that I shouldn't, and I know that it's stupid, but I take a small sip. "Not bad," I tell him. And really it's not bad. Okay, it's not good either. It tastes like paint thinner and orange juice.

"See," he says triumphantly as he takes a slug from his bottle of beer. "There's something for everyone."

I take another cautious sip, and this time it actually tastes a bit better. Still, I know I shouldn't drink it.

"I've seen you around school," he tells me.

I nod and act like it's the most normal thing in the world for me to be casually standing here drinking a screwdriver and conversing with someone like Slater Ross.

"Yeah, I've seen you around too," I say. "Looks like you guys have got a good track season going." Actually, I haven't been paying too much attention to the meets lately. Lucky for me, I get it right.

"Yeah, I just hope we can keep it going. But we've got the big meet with North next week, and they're ranked number three in the state."

"Yeah, that's right," I say, as if I follow these things closely.

"Are you going to come to the meet?"

"Yeah, sure," I tell him. "I'd *love* to see you run."

He kind of laughs. "Yeah, I've heard that line before." Then he makes this off-color joke about how girls like watching his backside as he sprints around the track.

I feel my cheeks redden as I nervously take another sip of my drink.

"But I'm sure you're not like that," he says. "I mean, being the daughter of a pastor and a church girl and all."

I shrug, somewhat surprised that he knows this about me. "Hey, I'm human too," I say.

He nods. "Yeah, maybe so."

But here's what's weird. By the time I finish the drink—and to my surprise, I do finish it—I feel all relaxed and loosened up. Not only that, but I feel this new sense of confidence. And suddenly it seems like maybe I do fit in with this crowd. I find myself laughing and joking with kids I would normally avoid, and I think I'm actually pretty hilarious. It seems the others think I'm funny too. It's like that one little screwdriver unveiled this whole new me.

"Want another one?" asks Slater, pointing to my empty glass.

Now, it's not as if I'm drunk—and really that's not my goal—but I honestly don't think one more little drink is going to turn me into a lush.

"Sure," I tell him, "why not?"

He grins and takes my glass. "Yeah, why not!"

three

OKAY, IT'S SUNDAY MORNING AND I AM TWO THINGS: (1) SLIGHTLY SICK, and (2) seriously freaked. I keep telling myself that I only had two screwdrivers last night, although I suspect I might have had more. To be honest, it's all kind of fuzzy. But I did wish that I could barf this morning. I've heard that makes you feel better when you have a hangover—not that I have a hangover exactly.

Okay, here's why I'm seriously freaked. I woke up early this morning and suddenly realized that I must've driven home last night. I mean, I sort of remember driving and taking Claire home and everything, but it's this blurry kind of memory, kind of like I dreamt the whole thing.

So I slipped outside to check on my car. I had imagined that it was all dented up, like maybe I ran into something and didn't even remember doing it. Or maybe I ran someone down and then just kept on going. It's a very freaky feeling, and I still cannot believe I actually got behind the wheel while I was "under the influence." Man, I could be in such trouble right now.

I carry these thoughts with me as I go to church. My mom's a little surprised that I want to ride with her, since I usually take my own car. As usual, my dad left a couple of hours ago. He practically lives at the church on Sundays.

"You feeling okay, honey?" she asks as she backs out of the driveway.

"I have a headache," I mutter as I look out the side window, "but I took something for it."

"Well, I hope you're not coming down with anything."

"Yeah, me too."

The rest of the ride is pretty quiet—well, except for the voice that is screaming inside my head. And it's not that still, small voice of God either. No, this is my own voice, and I'm yelling at myself and calling myself names like hypocrite, idiot, stupid jerk—you know, stuff like that. I'm just so angry with myself for being such a complete fool. Really, what was I thinking last night? I guess I wasn't thinking at all, and that's pretty scary.

I go straight to the youth house. It's early for Bible class, but I figure I might be able to make myself useful by setting up chairs. I guess I'm hoping this might act as some kind of penance to make up for last night's stupidity—not that our church believes in things like penance. And I've been a Christian long enough to know that the only way to remain in God's good grace is to confess my sins, receive Jesus' forgiveness, and "go and sin no more." But so far, I haven't taken those steps. I'm not even sure why not. Maybe it's because I still feel so guilty. Okay, I know that makes no sense—like if you feel guilty you should get your heart right before God. But it's like I'm embarrassed or something. Stupid, I know, but it's how I feel.

"How are you doing, Amber?" asks Glen as he sets some songbooks on the chairs I've just put out.

I kind of shrug. "I've been better."

He adjusts his dark-framed glasses, which give him this slightly nerdish look that Simi thinks is really attractive. Then he frowns as he studies me. "What's up?"

"Oh, I just have a headache is all," I say as I turn away and unfold another chair.

"Yeah, it's allergy season," he says. "Maybe that's it."

I nod. "Yeah, that's probably what it is."

"Amber Conrad!" scolds Simi. "What is going on with you?"

I turn and see her coming in. "New top?" I ask casually, hoping I can dodge this bullet. "It looks really good on you."

She smiles as she glances at the striped shirt. "Thanks. Actually it's Lena's. I just borrowed it." Now, Lena is Simi's older sister. She's already graduated from college, but she just moved back home, which I think is totally crazy.

"Must be nice having a sister to borrow clothes from," I say as I unfold another chair. "And one with good taste too."

"But back to you," says Simi, pointing her finger at me. "What was going on last night? And how come you never called me? And don't you ever check your cell phone messages?"

"Sorry," I tell her. "I'm not feeling so good. I think I have allergies or something."

She narrows her eyes, and I can tell she doesn't believe me. "Allergies?" she finally says. "Get real, Amber. I know something's up."

I glance around and notice a few other kids trickling in now. "Let's go outside," I say in a lowered voice.

So we head into the backyard and sit on one of the benches that are circled around the fire pit, where we sometimes have bonfires and roast hot dogs and marshmallows. I tell Simi about what happened last night, although I only admit to having "one drink." I'm not sure why I don't tell her the complete truth. Maybe it's pride.

"Amber, this is nuts," she tells me. "You are like totally losing it, girl."

"I know." I look down at my lap. "It was really lame. I know that."

"Then why'd you go? Why'd you drink again?"

I look back up at her, wishing I could somehow make her understand. "Because it was kinda fun," I say. "I mean, it was sort of exciting, you know? And after I had a drink, Slater Ross started talking to me and it was really pretty cool. I think he might even like me. He invited me to come to the track meet and—"

"Amber," she says in what sounds like a warning tone. "Can't you see that you are stepping over the line? I mean, seriously, this thing is going too far. You need to quit hanging with those kids."

"Why?"

"Because it's wrong. It's a sin, Amber."

"Hanging with those kids is a sin?" Now I'm getting mad. "So what would Jesus do, Simi?" I say in my most indignant voice. "Would he just turn his back on them?"

"But you're not changing them, Amber. They're changing you."

"That's not true. People can't change you. You can only change yourself. And maybe I need to change. Maybe I need to open my mind and start realizing that God loves everyone—even the kids who like to party."

"I'm not saying God doesn't love them."

"Well, maybe it's about time we started loving them too."

"Yeah, I'm sure you're right. We should love them, but that doesn't mean we need to go out and get wasted with them."

"Who said anything about being wasted?"

Now she throws up her hands and exhales loudly, her sign that we've reached her exasperation level. "Hey, all I'm saying is that you're playing with fire, Amber. And when you play with fire, you better expect to get burned."

"Yeah, whatever." I stand up. "We better get to Bible class."

"Yeah, I think you need someone to whack you upside the head with a big fat Bible."

"Thanks." I attempt a laugh as we walk across the yard.

"Seriously, Amber, you need to talk to God about this whole thing. Let him straighten you out."

I nod. "Yeah, you're right."

Then she pats me on the back and I think maybe we're okay—or mostly okay. To be honest, I feel like there's this little bit of a wall going up between us right now. I tell myself that it's just because I want to make new friends and break out of my old mold and stuff and that it's possible that Simi resents that or feels left out. But I also know that I haven't been completely truthful with her either. I suppose I haven't been completely truthful with myself, for that matter. But sometimes it's hard to know what's really true and what isn't. I guess I'm not sure.

Glen's teaching just seems to float right over my head this morning, and I'm not sure if it's the aftereffects of drinking last night or whether I'm just bored. But I use my good-church-kid expression that makes it appear as though I am listening and interested. (It even comes in handy during classes like biology or geometry.) Then it's time to walk across the parking lot and go to church for the worship service. I feel like I've done this a million times. It's as if I could do the whole thing with my eyes closed and never miss a step. I guess that would come in handy if I'm ever struck blind. Do people actually get struck blind anymore?

I sit in my regular spot in church: second row in the right-hand section. It's where a lot of us youth-group kids sit. We say it's to encourage my dad, but sometimes I think it's so we will look good, sort of holy or spiritual or something. Naturally, I go along with it.

That's what I do.

I feel like I've been a Christian my entire life. Sure, I remember the day when I actually stood up and went forward in church to give my heart to Jesus. It was December fourth and I had just turned seven. But in some ways, I think I'd really been a Christian even before that. I mean, I had always believed and had always said my prayers before bed. Going to the front of the church was more of a formality, I think—a kind of sealing of the deal.

But my parents had been very pleased and happy for me. My dad presented me with my own leather-bound Bible with my name in shiny gold letters. And I even got baptized with my older brother, James, just a week before Christmas. It was a big day for the Conrad family.

And while I do think it's sort of cool that I've been saved for most of my life, I guess I'm starting to wonder if I missed out on anything by spending all this time at church. I mean, it's not like I want to go out and smoke crack or have sex or pierce body parts or anything, but I guess I just want to have some fun.

I glance around the sanctuary and see Miss McAllister sitting in her regular spot (third row on the left). She smiles and waves at me just like she always does. She loves telling me about how her daddy was a "preacher man" too and how she literally grew up in this very church and has been here for as long as she can remember. Suddenly I wonder if that's what I'm going to be like someday. Will I end up with white hair and hands that shake, sitting in the same seat every Sunday and nodding off when the sermon runs too long? It's a frightening thought.

I really try to listen to my dad's sermon. Honestly, he's really a pretty good preacher, if I do say so myself, but it's like I just can't focus—like my brain is scrambled or maybe I've just heard the same words too many times before. And even worse, I start to feel trapped in here—kind of like I'm having this claustrophobia attack, like the walls are moving in and all the oxygen is getting sucked out of the air.

Okay, I know I'm being weird and slightly paranoid, not to mention melodramatic. But I'm seriously worried that my previous evening's consumption of alcohol may have actually damaged my brain. Is that even possible? And I keep telling myself that I should get on my knees and bow my head and really pray, that I should confess my sins to God and ask him to forgive me and cleanse me. For Pete's sake, I'm a preacher's kid—I know how this stuff is done. But it's like I just can't. It's like I'm stuck.

Here's what I think it is: I think I'm afraid to confess and repent because I have a funny feeling that I'm not over this—this whatever-it-is kind of thing. It's possible that I'm just going through a little rebellious period, something my mom might call a "phase"—I don't know for sure. But I think I'd be trying to fool myself (not to mention God) if I sat here and acted like I'm all sorry and repentant when I know that I am not. God can see right through that kind of stuff. Oh, crud. What am I gonna do?

four

I FEEL A VIBRATION IN MY PURSE AND REALIZE THAT MY CELL PHONE IS on, but at least it's in silent mode. I discreetly slip the phone out and sneak a peek at my caller ID to discover that it's Claire. I'm dying to know why she's calling me this morning and really wish I could answer it, but I also know that my dad would have a total fit if I did.

As soon as the service ends, I slip out a side door and quickly dial Claire's number. "What's up?" I ask.

"Just wondered if you wanted to go to the mall today," she says in a sleepy voice. "I feel the need to shop, and I heard that Nordstrom's just got in a bunch of Franco Sarto sandals. You in?"

"Sure," I tell her.

"Cool."

The idea of shoe shopping with Claire is enough to make the last remnants of my headache miraculously evaporate. It's like *presto change-o,* I am a new girl. Without explaining why, I beg a ride home from Simi and then tell my mom that I'm going to the mall. I know she assumes I'm going with Simi, and I guess it's no big deal.

"Why are you in such a hurry to get home?" Simi asks as she drives toward my house.

I shrug. "Just tired, I guess."

She kind of laughs. "Too much partying is my guess. Yeah, you better go home and sleep it off."

"What are you doing today?" I ask only to be polite.

"I told Lena I'd help her empty out her storage unit."

"So, she's really going to live at home, then?"

"I guess so. She said it's to save money."

"That makes sense. Speaking of money, are you still getting the job at The Caramel Corn Shoppe?"

"Yeah, and my aunt is still interested in hiring you too. Actually, I have to stop by today to sign some paperwork. Do you want me to talk to her for you?"

"Sure." I consider the fact that I'm going shopping with one of the richest girls I know today, and I immediately realize that spare cash might come in handy if I continue this friendship, not to mention that my dad would be hugely relieved if I started putting a little more toward my college fund. Just last week, he reminded me that the church academic scholarship (the one that everyone's so certain I'll receive) will *not* cover everything, not to mention that the private college I'm preregistered with isn't exactly cheap—not that I'm overly thrilled with the prospects of working at The Caramel Corn Shoppe. I mean, who wants to go around smelling like burnt sugar and candy all day? But at least it's a job and I can continue it into the summer and my dad should be happy. And fortunately the shop is located in a relatively uncool strip mall where it's very unlikely that we'll see anyone we know from school.

"I'm going to start this week, but Aunt Jan said she was going to let another girl go and will want to hire a replacement really soon."

"Why's she firing everyone?"

"She says they're irresponsible. They give stuff away and take too long of breaks—things like that." Simi laughs. "And even though

Aunt Jan's not a Christian, she's decided that it might be safer to hire Christians."

"Well, tell her to give me a call." We're at my house now. "And thanks for the ride. Have fun helping Lena." But I make a face that suggests unloading a storage unit really sounds like a drag.

"Yeah, thanks a lot."

As I go into the house, I experience this uncomfortable feeling. I can't quite describe it, but I think it's conflicted, like I'm kind of torn. I mean, I really like Simi and she's been the best friend, but at the same time, it's like I'm being deceitful to her—and I feel guilty, almost like I'm cheating on her. Now, *that* is seriously twisted. How can you cheat on a girlfriend?

I tell myself that I'm making this into something it's not and then hurry to my room to change. The problem is, when I look in my closet, everything looks blah and boring. It's like I honestly don't have a thing to wear. At times like these, I wish I had an older sister to bum clothes from. But all I have is an older brother, and he's off at college—as if I'd ever want to borrow any of James' preppy clothes.

I finally settle on my favorite cargo pants and a white T-shirt and a relatively new black hoodie sweatshirt. I guess it's kind of my classic look. Simi is always telling me that classic is my best style. Of course, I always tell her that's just because I am so average-looking. I mean, I'm average height, average build, and I have average-looking medium-brown hair that's straight and blunt-cut just below my shoulders. I had just been considering getting highlights, but Simi informed me that she'd read that "mat is back" in a fashion mag, which means that you shouldn't highlight your hair now. Well, whatever.

At least my eyes are good, or so people say. They are big and brown, and my eyelashes are thick and dark enough that I don't even bother wearing mascara. Simi says she'd kill to have my eyelashes, although I think hers actually look better, but then she really piles on the mascara. But she can get away with that sort of thing, being tall and thin and rather dramatic-looking with her exotic Italian good looks. Maybe that's one reason that I'm open to having a different friend. Maybe it'll make me look better.

I know, I know—that sounds totally shallow. But the truth is, I sometimes feel overshadowed by Simi's beauty. It's like when we're together, everyone is looking at her and I feel practically invisible. Of course, she doesn't think this is true, but then I don't know anyone who's less aware of their own beauty than Simi.

Honestly, I can't understand why she's not more popular—but then popularity is a rather mysterious trait to me. I mean, it doesn't seem to have as much to do with being the smartest or prettiest or most talented as it does with knowing the "right" people. And how does one get to know the right people? Like I've said, it's a mystery to me. Popularity always has been, but for some reason I am drawn like a magnet to it. Why is that? And for some reason I want to get to know Claire better, even though I suspect she's kind of using me right now—her ticket to get out of the house with someone her mom considers "safe." But then that's what I am, I guess: safe. At least I used to be.

When I get to Claire's house, I go ring the doorbell and tell myself not to stand there gaping at her beautiful house.

The door opens. "Amber," says Claire's mother with a smile. "How are you doing?" Her blonde hair is pulled back in a smooth kind of twist, and she has on a crisp white shirt and khakis—some expensive designer, I'm sure. Very sleek and sophisticated.

I smile back. "Great," I tell her.

"Did you go to church this morning?" she asks, and for some reason, this feels like a test.

I nod. "Yep. It's kind of an expected thing, you know, when your dad's the pastor, you better be at church or have a really good reason why you're not."

She kind of laughs. "Well, I happen to think that's nice."

"Do you go to church?" I ask, suddenly feeling stupid for doing so.

Her brows twist slightly. "I, uh, I used to—before I got married, that is. Now we're gone so much and my husband travels for work. And, well, it's hard to give up a Sunday, you know."

I nod as if I do know, but really I don't. I mean, I cannot imagine what it would feel like to have the luxury of skipping out on church if I wanted to. It's just not done in my family.

"Hey, Amber," calls Claire as she comes down the stairs. "I didn't know you were here." Claire is wearing a pale pink top and Capri pants, and her blonde hair is pulled back and tied with a scarf. She looks older than usual and quite cosmopolitan. Suddenly I wish I'd worn something a little more fashionable.

"Have fun, you two," calls Claire's mom. "Don't buy out the store."

"You look nice," I tell Claire as we go outside.

"So do you," she says in an unconvincing voice.

I shrug. "No, I don't." I shake my head. "When it comes to fashion, well, I'm not sure I really get it."

She laughs. "Well, you're with the right person, then. Fashion is my thing."

Now, this makes me truly curious, but I don't really know how to ask why someone as popular and fashionable as Claire is interested in hanging with me. Then I remember her mom and her DUI and it sort of makes sense again.

She chatters about fashion as I drive to the mall, but I am

feeling increasingly uncomfortable and suddenly it's like I can't stand it anymore. I park my car in the underground parking and then turn to Claire. "Okay, I know this is going to sound lame, but I'm curious about something."

She blinks her blue eyes at me and looks confused. "What? What's bugging you?"

"It's just that you and I are, well, you know, really different from one another. And it was really sweet of you to invite me to Tommy's party on Friday, and then it was fun hanging with you last night, but I guess I'm wondering what's up with this? I mean, do you really consider me your friend, or am I just an easy ride?"

Okay, now, I'm looking at her expression—a mixture of hurt and confusion—and I just don't know why I did this. I mean, why couldn't I have just kept my big mouth shut and enjoyed the ride? Why have I thrown all my cards on the table and put this whole thing at risk? Maybe I'm just stupid.

She sighs and seems to consider her answer. "Do you want the truth, Amber?"

I swallow and nod.

"Well, you're right. I know we're in kind of different circles and stuff, but the thing is, my old friends and I, well, we're just not that close anymore. I mean, Stacy is always with Aaron, like she can't let him out of her sight for a minute. And then there's Megan—my so-called best friend—but she won't even speak to me."

"Why's that?"

"Let's just say we've had a little disagreement."

"Oh. What about Haley Banks?"

Claire shrugs. "She's okay, I guess."

Now I consider this. "So then are you saying that you actually do want to be friends?" I ask, knowing I sound totally lame. "I mean, I'm not just a convenient ride and someone your mom will approve of?"

She laughs. "Oh, is that it?"

"Yeah, sort of."

"Okay, I'll admit that has its pluses, but I like you, Amber. I know you're more academic than I am and quieter—usually anyway. But you really loosen up after a drink or two. That's when the fun Amber comes out."

That kind of makes me smile, but it also makes me feel a little uncomfortable—or maybe just insecure.

"Speaking of that . . ." She gets this mischievous look on her face now. Then she digs around in her bag until she emerges with a small silver flask.

"What is that?"

She puts her forefinger to her lips as if someone might actually be able to hear us although we're still sitting in my car. "It's our secret." Then she opens the flask and takes a big swig.

Well, I'm not sure what I think about this. I mean, isn't there some kind of law about not having alcohol in your car? But the next thing I know, she's handing it to me.

"No, uh, that's okay."

"Come on, Amber," she urges. "Just one little drink?" Then she giggles. "Don't be a party pooper."

So, despite all the warning signals going off inside me, I take the flask and have a drink. But man, whatever's inside that flask tastes like poison to me and I'm sputtering and coughing and my eyes are watering and my throat is on fire. "What is *in* that thing?" I demand when I am finally able to speak.

"Just a little Jack." She laughs even louder now.

"Huh?"

"Jack Daniel's."

"What is that?"

"Whiskey, silly."

"Oh."

Then, without even blinking, she takes another chug, secures the lid, and gets out of the car. But as soon as we're out, she's popping a breath mint into her mouth. "Want one?"

"I guess." Although I'm not sure. Maybe her breath mints are spiked too. But it turns out to be just an ordinary mint, although my poor burnt tongue is still sensitive and burning and I wonder if my sense of taste will ever be the same. One thing I know: Jack Daniel's and I do not seem to get along too well and I'll be just as pleased if I never make his acquaintance again. Still, I am curious as to Claire's ability to gulp that stuff the way she does. I think I know why they call it "firewater" now.

But thoughts of alcohol and silver flasks quickly fade as we peruse the aisles and shelves at Nordstrom's, and I quickly discover that Claire really *does* know her stuff about fashion. The only problem is that she has very expensive taste. And while she has what appears to be a limitless credit card, my funds are not quite so plentiful. I mean, I do have a bank account as well as a debit card (my dad made me open one when I was sixteen so that I could learn to handle money), and because I've worked off and on, and do a fairly decent job of saving my allowance, I do have a little bit of money in it—but not enough to keep up with someone like Claire. And definitely not in a store like Nordstrom's. I can't believe the way Claire is spending money—or rather, "charging it." But it is kind of interesting trailing her and seeing how well she knows her way around this store. And she tries to tempt me into getting a really cool pair of sandals—well, until I see the price. Then it's like *forget it.*

Even so, I do manage to find a greatly reduced sales rack in the back of the junior section, and although Claire's initial reaction is to shun the whole idea, she eventually gives in—but only after she spies me holding up this tangerine-colored shirt.

"Definitely not *that* color," she says with an expression that suggests I have just picked up roadkill. "But how about this?" She pulls out a pale yellow shirt in the same design. "I think this would look good on you."

I hold up the shirt, and she nods with satisfaction and then returns to pawing through the rack. "Okay, maybe we can find a few treasures in here after all."

When it's all said and done, Claire actually admits that she enjoyed my bargain shopping almost as much as buying with no regard to the price tag. And as we leave the store, I am contemplating Claire's incredible fashion sense, not to mention her credit card, when I spot two familiar figures across the way—Simi and Lena—and I have no desire to bump into them right now.

"Wanna get something to eat?" I say, turning quickly toward the food court and hoping that Simi hasn't seen me yet. I know it's silly and immature and extremely rude, but it's like I can't help myself. I just don't want to have to explain this.

five

"I CAN'T BELIEVE HOW MUCH STUFF YOU BOUGHT," I SAY AS WE WALK away from Simi and Lena. "Hey, do you want me to carry one of those bags for you?"

"Thanks." She hands me the big shopping bag with two pairs of sandals in it, and suddenly I feel rather important, like here I am carrying not one but two Nordstrom's bags. Stupid, but true.

"I didn't really mean to buy that much," she admits as we get closer to the food court. "Sometimes I just can't help myself."

"Hey, it looks like fun to me."

She laughs. "Well, that's a way better attitude than Haley or Stacy have. They usually get mad at me."

"For buying stuff? Maybe they're jealous."

"Yeah, maybe."

We enter the food court now and I casually glance over my shoulder to make sure that Simi and Lena aren't right behind us. I'm relieved to see that they're not.

"You know, one of the main reasons I spend so much money is to get back at my stepdad," says Claire as we stand and look at the variety of restaurants.

"Why?"

"Well, I don't think my mom would've married Mike if he

hadn't been so loaded, so I guess I kinda resent Mr. Big Bucks and I figure I should take it out on his bank account—kinda like it's all his fault that my parents never got the chance to get back together, you know?"

"Oh."

"Going on a spending spree is like my way of getting even with him."

I kind of laugh. "And he doesn't mind?"

"He complains sometimes, but mostly I don't think he really notices."

"Lucky you." I follow her into the pizza line, relieved that she picked pizza and not some stupid health food. Simi always goes for things with vegetables and tofu. But just give me a hot cheesy piece of pizza and a Dr Pepper, and I'm good.

Once we've gotten our pizza and drinks and are seated at the table, I notice Claire discreetly slipping out her flask again. She keeps it below the table, but I know what she's doing. We're sitting in a corner and her back is to the crowd, but I still can't believe her nerve as she opens the flask and pours that stuff into her Coke. I mean, what if a security guard saw her? Would he call the police and have us arrested? The whole thing is making me seriously nervous, and I'm not sure I can even eat now.

"What are you doing?" I finally hiss as she puts the top back on the flask.

But she just laughs and drops the flask back into her bag. "No biggie, Amber. Really, just chill. No one ever notices this kind of thing."

"You mean you do this all the time?"

She just shrugs. "Not *all* the time. Just when I need something to relax me." Then she looks back up at me with a twinkle in her eye.

"Hey, what's the matter? You jealous or something? You want me to put some Jack in your drink too?"

I shake my head. "No, thanks. I take my Dr Pepper straight up, thank you very much."

I try to act as if I'm not still in shock, and when I realize that Claire is probably right and that the security guard probably doesn't care if kids are getting drunk at the mall, I start to lighten up. But I do notice that Claire seems more interested in her beverage than in her pizza.

"Aren't you hungry?" I finally ask after I've polished off my pizza.

She shrugs. "To be honest, I'm feeling kinda bummed right now."

"Really?" I lean forward with interest. "What's wrong?"

"Well, I wasn't going to say anything because it's really no big deal, but Tommy and I broke up last night."

I blink. "You did? Man, I could've sworn I saw you guys kissing last night."

"Yeah, well, that was earlier on, and you were slightly out of it when the actual event happened. I decided not to burden you with it while you drove me home. To be honest, I thought you needed to concentrate on your driving."

"Was I really that bad?" I feel slightly horrified again. I mean, to think I was driving the streets of Ashton almost totally wasted. Man, it makes me feel kind of sick inside.

"No, you were driving okay, but I sure didn't want you to get pulled over. Mostly you were driving pretty slow and just being really cautious, but cops watch for that too. It gets their attention."

I sigh deeply. "Man, I'm so glad I didn't get stopped."

"Yeah, it's a bummer getting caught and losing your license. That might even have something to do with Tommy wanting to break up with me. He was always all worried that I was going to do something crazy. I mean, talk about your double standards. He drinks and everything, but he claims he's got it all under control." She rolls her eyes. "Yeah, right."

"So that's why you guys broke up?"

"I don't know. Maybe it was just something that needed to happen. I mean, we'd been talking about it for a while, and it really was mutual."

"Then why are you so bummed?"

"I guess it just feels like the end of an era or something. You know, Tommy and I have been together most of our senior year." She uses her napkin to wipe her eyes.

Now I actually feel sorry for her. "So, are you going to be okay?"

She sniffs and looks down. "Yeah, I guess so." Then she looks back at me with red, watery eyes. "Do you mind if I have another drink?"

I kind of shrug. I mean, I really do mind, but I feel badly for her and don't want to say no. And once again, she is slipping out her flask and pouring some into her Coke. "Want some?" she asks hopefully. "It's really pathetic to drink alone."

Well, I know I should say no and that I should discourage her from doing this as well, but for some reason, I don't. Instead I shove my half-full cup over to her and then watch over her shoulder—out toward where people are milling about and eating and basically ignoring us—as she discreetly pours some of her firewater into my cup.

After returning her flask to her purse, she slides back my cup and lifts hers in what looks like a toast. "To good friends," she says.

I halfheartedly lift my cup and echo her.

"And to new beginnings," she says before taking a sip from her straw.

I'm not sure if I really want to taste that dreadful stuff again, but it seems she's waiting, so I take a very tentative and small sip. To my surprise, it's not nearly as bad as before. I guess the Dr Pepper helps to cover the taste. Even so, it does not taste good, and now I don't enjoy my soda nearly as much as I would have. Even so, I manage to finish it off, and it's not long before I'm feeling a little giddy.

"I can't believe I did that," I admit as we gather our bags and get ready to leave.

She pats me on the back and giggles. "It'll be *our* little secret." But the word *secret* sounds more like *sheecret*. Of course, I don't mention this, and I don't mention that it looks like she's walking slightly crooked. For all I know, I may be doing the same. We walk around the mall awhile longer, making jokes and laughing loudly, and I lighten up and actually begin to have fun.

"Amber!" calls a familiar voice, and I turn to see Simi and Lena coming out of one of those stores that has all kinds of storage things. Simi's carrying a stack of baskets, and Lena has a large box.

I wave and continue walking.

"Hey, wait!" calls Simi as she hurries to catch up with us. "You didn't say you were going to the mall today."

"Neither did you."

"Well, we finished emptying Lena's storage unit, but she wanted some stuff to store things in."

Then Simi pauses to introduce Lena to Claire. But even as she does this, I can tell that she's looking closely at Claire, sort of sizing her up. Next Claire is complimenting Lena on her jacket when Simi leans over and quietly asks me, "What's up with you two?"

"Huh?" I say stupidly.

Then Simi gets this slightly horrified look. "Have you been drinking?" she whispers.

I step back, remembering that Claire and I forgot to chase our sodas with mints, but I shake my head. "No. We just had pizza at the food court."

Simi does not look convinced. "Come on," she says to Lena. "We better go if you still want to hit Pottery Barn."

Lena smiles and waves at us. Then Claire and I continue down the mall.

"Lena is nice," says Claire, "but honestly, I don't know what you see in Simi. I mean, she's pretty and everything, but she seems so boring, don't you think?"

"She can be kinda stuck in her ways," I admit. What an understatement. I mean, if Simi had *her* way, we'd all be stuck in her ways. Like it's her way or the highway. I wish she'd just lighten up.

"I'm getting tired," says Claire. "Want to go now? We can hang at my house for a while. I think Mom and Mike had plans for the afternoon, so we should have the place to ourselves."

"Cool," I say, and we head to the car. Okay, I'm a little concerned about driving under the influence, but actually I don't feel the least bit impaired—not like I was last night. In fact, if anything, I'm thinking more clearly than usual. And as I drive, we talk nonstop and I feel like I'm wittier than ever. And hey, I'm really having fun.

Claire is right. Her mom and Mike have gone out, and according to the note, they won't be home until late. Claire is excited. "We could have a party!" she says suddenly. "We could call up some friends and—"

"Seriously, Claire," I cut her off. "Do you think that's a good idea? You just got out of being grounded, and your mom seems pretty concerned about what you're doing. Don't you think having a party might really mess things up?"

She considers this. "You know, you could be right." Then she smiles. "See, you are a good influence on me. Want a tour of *Mike's* house?"

"Sure." And so she is taking me from one room to the next, and it's pretty impressive. "What does Mike do?" I finally ask.

"He's an investment counselor."

"Wow, he must be pretty good at it."

"Yeah, I guess. Or else he just tricks people into handing over their money. I'm not really sure."

We end up outside by the pool, but it's not really warm enough to go swimming. "This is pretty," I tell her as I sit down on a thickly padded lounge chair and lean back. "Lifestyles of the rich and famous."

She laughs. "Yeah, whatever." Then she flips a switch, and music starts coming through the outdoor speakers. "All the comforts of home," she says as she takes off her sandals and dips her feet in the pool. "Hey, ya want a drink?"

"Sure," I say and then realize that she probably means an alcoholic drink.

She grins and stands. "Cool. I know just where to get something."

I start to protest and then decide not to. Instead, I just follow her back in the house. Now I'm thinking, surely her mom wouldn't go off and leave any kind of alcohol in the house—not if she's as worried about Claire as she seems. Claire leads us to the billiards room, where I previously noticed a large bar area but no bottles within sight. "They keep it locked," she explains as she reaches up to a deep green vase on a high shelf. Then she takes down the vase and reaches inside, pulling out a shiny brass key. "But I have my own key," she says as she puts the vase back.

"They gave you your own key?"

She laughs. "Well, not exactly, but it's not hard to have a duplicate made." Then she goes around to the back side of the bar, opens it up, and says, *"Voilà!"*

I look over her shoulder to see bottles and bottles of all kinds of alcohol. It looks like something out of a movie or TV show. Honestly, I never realized that ordinary people kept this kind of stuff in their homes. But then, I was raised as a preacher's kid, and Claire's family seems anything but ordinary. I watch as she takes out a bottle of something clear and something gold-colored. The label on the clear bottle says Smirnoff, and I realize that it's vodka.

"Aren't you a screwdriver girl?" she asks.

I shrug, unsure that I really want another drink. I mean, what's going on here? And why do I allow myself to do what I know to be wrong?

"Well, you need to learn another drink," she tells me. "Screwdrivers are sort of old-fashioned, not to mention cliché. How about a Sea Breeze?"

"What's that?"

"Trust me, you'll like it."

So she mixes some ingredients, mostly fruit juices from what I can see, and hands me a pinkish drink in a cool-shaped glass. "Is this a martini glass?" I ask, feeling stupid.

She nods and then takes out a squat tumbler and adds ice and then some alcohol—and that's all. She doesn't even put in soda or juice or anything. "Bottoms up," she says, and before I know it, her drink is gone.

"Come on," she urges me. "You gotta keep up. This isn't a party of one, you know."

So I sample my drink, and it's actually not too bad. I think I might even like it better than the screwdriver. And before I can protest, she's made me another one and she's pouring what I think is her third one. "Want to take these poolside?" she asks.

"Sounds good."

So we go back outside and I take off my shoes and we both put our feet in the water. I'm surprised at how warm it is. "This is nice," I say as I wiggle my toes. "I think I could get used to this."

"Drinks by the pool," she says in a slightly sloshy voice. "Now, if we only had a cute pool boy to bring them to us."

"Yeah." I laugh and make a lame attempt to snap my fingers. "Bring us another one, pool boy!"

SIX

FALLING INTO THE POOL WITH YOUR CLOTHES ON TENDS TO SOBER YOU up rather quickly. And I suppose it didn't help that Claire was laughing her head off from her high spot on the dry deck. I climbed out in a soggy heap and tried to act like I thought it was funny, but the truth is, I think she pushed me. I think. Who can know for sure?

"I should go," I tell her as I remove my hoodie sweatshirt and attempt to wring it out. I wring and twist it until the relatively new sweatshirt looks like a misshapen mess that an orangutan might appreciate. The air is cool enough that I'm shivering now, and all I want to do is go home and go to bed. I seriously hope I haven't consumed enough alcohol to impair my driving or give me a hangover tomorrow morning.

Claire is still laughing as she hands me a big thick towel. Apparently, she's unaware that there are signs of partying (like a few empty martini glasses and tumblers and these funny paper umbrellas that she put in our last drinks) here and there. I mean, what if her mom and stepdad came home right now? I look at the outdoor clock and see that it's nearly six and realize that my family will wonder where I am.

"Don't you think we should clean up a little?" I ask. But Claire is in another world now. She's flat on her back on a chaise lounge and talking nonsense to herself. I can't even make out the words. Feeling guilty, I know I should do something. But what?

So, wrapped in a towel and feeling like a headless chicken, I rush around the pool area picking up glasses and stuff and carrying it all into the bar area. I wonder if I'll have to wash the glasses by hand before I return them to their proper places, but I'm pleasantly surprised to see a small dishwasher built right into the bar, and it's already half-filled with glasses and things. Our little contribution probably won't even be noticed.

So I put the glasses in and then give the granite countertop a quick wipe-down. Then I lock the liquor cabinet and remove the key and restore it to its hiding place in the green vase. I feel like I've just run a marathon. Suddenly Claire appears.

"Here's shome dry clothes," she says as she holds out some sweats. Swaying unsteadily, she holds on to the bar to brace herself and then smiles. "Things are starting to shpin."

"Careful," I warn her, and then I grab the sweats and head for the dressing room that's near the pool. After I'm changed and dry, I wrap my wet clothes in the pool towel and emerge feeling somewhat victorious. "Thanks, Claire," I say. "And I'll bring back your towel late—"

"Don' worry about it," she says in her sloshy voice as she waves her hand. "We got losh of 'em."

"You better get some rest," I tell her as I head for the front door.

"Tha's right," she says as she reaches the stairs and holds onto the banister as if it's a lifeline. "Tha's zactly what I'm gonna do."

Okay, now, here's what's weird. As I get into my car, I imagine a drunken Claire falling down the stairs and knocking herself out. I mean, the image is so clear that I almost go back inside the house.

But I don't. Instead, I actually pray for her. How weird is that? Here I am, doing what I know is *not* pleasing to God and I am praying for Claire. I think I am seriously demented.

I tell myself that I'm sober as I carefully drive toward home. I mean, that dunk in the pool was a real shock, sort of like a wake-up call. And I've heard that people can get sobered by something like that. But even as I tell myself this, I'm not entirely sure. And I worry that I'm driving too cautiously and perhaps, like Claire said, I might be attracting the attention of a patrol car. By the time I reach my street, I am so nervous that I'm actually sweating, but I look behind me and to my relief see no flashing red and blue lights coming after me. It seems I have made it home free again. Remembering the incident at the mall, I ransack my purse for a breath mint and manage to come up with a solitary Lifesaver that's been rolling around at the bottom for who knows how long. Then before I get out of my car, I pull out my sunglasses and slip them on. Okay, I realize it's not even sunny, but I also suspect that my eyes look as bloodshot as Claire's by now.

As I walk to my house, I wonder if perhaps God is watching out for me. Oh, I know I'm blowing it, but then my dad is always the one who says that God is always ready to forgive us, that God is our loving Father who wants only the best for us, and I'm thinking, *Okay, maybe God understands this thing I'm going through. Maybe he is protecting me and watching over me.* But even as I think these thoughts, I know that I'm just being ridiculous. I mean, seriously, why would God watch out for someone who was messing up on purpose?

"Where have you been?" asks Mom as I attempt to slip in the back door. I keep a safe distance from her olfactory radar and pretend to be absorbed with putting my keys into my purse.

"At Claire's," I tell her. "We went there after the mall."

"Who's Claire?" asks Mom. "I thought you were with Simi."

"Simi had to help Lena move some stuff. And actually we did meet up with them at the mall, but afterward we went to Claire's."

She frowns at my hair now. "Why is your hair wet?"

I kind of laugh. "I fell into Claire's pool."

"Really?"

"Yeah, it was pretty funny. We were just acting silly, and the next thing I knew, I was all wet. Claire loaned me her sweats."

"But why the sunglasses, Amber? And in the house?"

"They'd just put chlorine in the pool," I magically come up with. "It's irritating my eyes."

"There's some Visine in the medicine cabinet," she says as if my answers have satisfied her, but then it's like she remembers something. "But really, Amber, who is this Claire? Have I met her before? Does she go to church?"

"Claire Phillips. She's a friend from school. She doesn't go to church, but she's going through some hard stuff," I say quickly. "And she may be getting more open to church."

"What kind of *hard* stuff?"

"Like she doesn't get along that well with her stepdad, and her boyfriend just broke up with her. She's kinda bummed. I'm just trying to be there for her, you know? And her mom likes that I go to church, and I'm thinking of inviting Claire to come too."

Mom smiles now. I've dealt her the Christian card, and she's happy to pick it up. "Well, that's really nice," she says. "I'm so happy to hear about people who are reaching out to others. Good for you, Amber. And tell Claire that I'd like to meet her sometime."

I nod. "Yeah, I'm sure she'd like to meet you too."

And so that's it. I think I am off the hook and passed whatever kind of test that was meant to be.

"Dad and I are having dinner with our Bible-study group tonight," she calls after me. "But there's leftover spaghetti in the fridge if you're hungry."

"Thanks, Mom." But as I head down the hall, I'm thinking spaghetti or any kind of food sounds gross right now. In fact, my stomach is a mess. I'm not sure if it's the result of alcohol or all the stress I felt while driving home. I make a stop in the bathroom across from my bedroom while telling myself that I don't want to keep drinking like that. It's stupid and risky and makes me sick. Yet even as I say these things, I'm not sure that I'm really listening. I have a feeling that I'm going to hurl, and worried that Mom will hear and come rushing in here, I lock the door and turn the shower on, hoping the sound of water will disguise the noise.

I take in some shaky breaths and try to steady myself as I sit on the edge of the bathtub. I wrap my arms around my sides and wish that I hadn't drunk so much. I had really intended to just have one drink. But then Claire kept playing bartender and pool boy and, well, I'm not sure how many I finally had. Maybe I thought the fruit juice might've helped. But suddenly the mere thought of fruit juice is totally disgusting. I feel hot and then cold and then hot again. And the next thing I know, I am hugging the toilet and throwing up like my guts are trying to come out. Or maybe it's my brain that I'm barfing out—I'm not sure. But by the time I'm finished, I feel as wrung out as my hoodie sweatshirt, and I am crying too. I know this is a miserable way to live, and I know I've blown it, but even so, I'm not sure that I'm ready to end this thing. What on earth is wrong with me?

Since the water is still running in the shower and I can tell that I'm reeking of chlorine and who knows what else, I decide I might as well hop in. I guess I'm hoping I can wash away all the crud that seems to be clinging to me right now. I turn the water on extra hot, thinking maybe I can burn the badness out of me with some kind of pseudoholy fire. And then I just stand there as it runs and runs. I stand there so long that the water eventually gets cool, and I quickly turn it off. My dad hates it when anyone uses up all the hot water. He says it's not only wasteful but also bad for our old water heater. Well, I hope I haven't done any permanent damage.

I get out of the shower and step into a cloud of white mist. It's like the whole bathroom is underwater now, and it's so blurry that I wonder if I may still be under the effect of alcohol, like maybe I'll see a pink elephant trotting by next. But then I tell myself that most of the alcohol has probably been flushed down the toilet. I turn on the fan and dry myself off, rubbing and rubbing as if I can rub my mistakes away.

I'm fairly sure my parents have left the house by now, but I just barely open the door and listen to be sure. The house is silent and so I think the coast is probably clear. With the towel wrapped around me, I dash to my bedroom and close the door. When I see myself in the full-length mirror, I am shocked. It's like I'm not even me. At first I am horrified that I can look so awful, but then it's like I'm fascinated too.

My skin is red and puffy-looking. I'm sure this has as much to do with my scalding hot shower as the alcohol, but it definitely is not attractive. My face is also red and puffy, and my eyes (usually my best asset) are bloodshot and watery. Not only that but I have these odd little spots around my eyes and I'm not even sure what that is about. All I know is that I look extremely ugly—frighteningly ugly. And so I turn off the light, pull on a T-shirt and boxers, and climb into bed. I have no idea what I'll look (or feel) like in the morning, but I really wish I could sleep for about a week. I wonder if I can pass myself off as sick tomorrow. Maybe I really am sick.

I tell myself to pray—to confess my sins and ask forgiveness—but I am unable to do this. I guess I've always been a little on the stubborn side. My dad says it's a good thing when your stubbornness helps you to remain true to God. But if it goes the other way, well, you better watch out.

I don't know how long I'm asleep, but the sound of something ringing wakes me up and I groggily reach for my cell phone. It's like I don't know exactly where I am or how I got here. My heart is pounding like it wants out of my chest as I answer the phone and realize it's Simi.

"What is going on with you?" she demands in an angry sounding voice. "I tried to reach you on your cell earlier today and you didn't answer. And I've tried your house all night, but no one seemed to be home. Is everything okay?"

"Yeah," I say as I sit up and rub my aching head. "I was asleep."

"Asleep or passed out?"

"Real funny."

"Come on, Amber, I'm not stupid. Both you and Claire reeked of alcohol. What had you been doing? Bar hopping?"

"Yeah, you bet. Like there are so many bars that let eighteen-year-olds come inside and drink."

"Whatever. But seriously, Amber, what are you thinking? Are you really becoming an alcoholic? It's like you're changing almost overnight. I've heard it's like that with alcoholics—like they take one drink and then it's all over."

"Get real, Simi. I'm not an alcoholic."

"Really?"

"Yeah."

"Well, tell me, how much did you drink today?"

"I don't know."

"Right."

Her voice is so full of judgment and condemnation that I'm about ready to hang up.

"And how much did you drink last night?"

"None of your business."

"And the night before?"

"Simi!" I'm really getting irritated now.

"You go to a drinking party on Friday, then you skip out on youth group to go drinking again on Saturday, and then I see you at the mall on Sunday—right after church—and you and your new buddy are plastered."

"We were *not* plastered."

"Whatever."

"And this isn't any of your business anyway. You're just like those Pharisees who were always picking on Jesus. They said he was a glutton and a drunkard."

"This isn't anything like that, Amber."

"How would you know?"

There's a pause, and her voice softens just slightly. "Because I care about you, and I'm worried. Graduation is so close, and you're up for that scholarship and—"

"The scholarship is in the bag."

"But I don't like what you're doing to yourself, Amber, and I think you should—"

"Look, Simi, I know you don't understand this, but I'm only hanging with Claire to help her. She's really having some problems, and I think she's starting to trust me. I'm hoping that—"

"She just wants a new drinking buddy," says Simi in that I-know-everything voice.

"That's not true."

"Oh, yeah? Why do you think all her friends have dumped her? They're fed up, Amber. She's a mess, and everyone knows it."

"You don't know her, Simi. And you have no right to judge her like that."

"Hey, I'm just calling a spade a spade."

"And what's that supposed to mean?"

"Maybe you should figure it out."

I sigh. "Simi, I don't want to fight with you. You're my best friend, and I kind of need a friend right now."

"I'm trying to be a good friend," she says in a sincere voice. "I just don't know how to help you."

"Maybe you can help by believing in me—by being a good listener, by not being so critical of Claire and making such outrageous accusations. She's really struggling, you know."

Simi is quiet for a second. "Okay, okay—you're probably right. The truth is, I might just be jealous. But even so, I don't think it's right for you to drink with her."

"I know, I know. And I know you're right about that too."

"Really?"

"Yeah. I can admit I let it go too far, but it's hard spending time with someone and getting them to trust you. It just gets kind of confusing." Okay, even as I say this, I can smell the insincerity of it. It's like I know that I'm just trying to make Simi believe in me. Maybe I'm afraid she'll blow my cover to the youth-group kids and that my parents will find out, but it's like I suddenly need Simi to trust me again.

"So you're really not going over the deep end in this drinking and partying thing?"

"No. I'm just trying to be a light in the darkness."

Then there's a long pause. "Well, I guess I should try to do that too. I'll try to be nicer to Claire," she says, "and kids like her."

"Cool."

"Yeah, I guess I was being too judgmental with you. I just naturally assumed the worst, Amber. I'm sorry."

"Hey, it's understandable. And I forgive you." Okay, I almost choke on that. I mean, how ironic it is that I'm sitting here saying I forgive her, when *I'm* the one who's screwing up. I mean, how twisted is that? Really, I am pathetic.

So we talk some more, and she seems totally reassured and okay about me now, and that makes me feel more guilty than ever. Like, how am I going to live this thing down? But after I hang up the phone, I tell myself that things are going to change. I simply experienced a crazy three-day drinking binge, but it's finished and done now. This will be the end of it.

But even as I tell myself this, I'm not entirely sure I believe it. As a matter of fact, I think I'm turning into a big fat liar!

seven

To my surprise I wake up very early. The sun's not even up. And I actually feel perfectly fine. What a relief. I'm thinking, *Today is the first day of the rest of my life*, just like what the dorky poster in my dad's office says. And I'm going to straighten up and start acting the way that I know God wants me to act. I'm done with the crazy drinking thing—for sure.

So I get up and dig through my bag to find a couple of assignments that I neglected to do this weekend and flop down on my bed and get right to them. It's weird how it feels kind of good to do schoolwork, like it makes my life seem normal again. And after I finish and go take a shower and get dressed, I actually start to wonder if the strange events of the last three days even happened. Then my cell phone rings.

"Hey, Amber," says Claire. "How's it going?"

"Okay." I shove my notebook into my bag, which I hoist over my shoulder.

"Do you think I could bum a ride off you today? My mom left early for work, and, well, I'm not speaking to Michael at the moment."

I consider this and then wonder if I should just blow her off. I mean, it seems like every time I'm with Claire, I start heading for trouble. And yet I know that's not fair. It's not like she forces me to drink. Besides, I rationalize, how can I possibly be enticed to imbibe at this hour of the morning? It just seems crazy.

"Sure," I tell her. "I'll be there in about fifteen minutes."

I grab an apple and head out the door, pausing to let Mom know that I'm giving Claire a ride to school.

"That's nice," she says with a smile.

Yeah, I'm thinking that *is* nice. And God certainly can't have a problem with my helping out a friend. Even so, I feel a little uneasy.

"Get over yourself," I say into the rearview mirror as I back out of the driveway.

Claire must've spotted my car from the house because she comes out as soon as I pull up. She has on these big dark glasses with plastic frames, and her face looks paler than usual. I wonder if she got sick last night too.

"How are you feeling?" I ask as she climbs in.

"Wiped out," she says as she leans back and sighs deeply. "Sometimes I think this school year will never end."

"Did you get sick last night?" I ask.

"Sick?" She turns and peers at me through her sunglasses. "What do you mean?"

"I mean from drinking too much."

She just laughs. "Not hardly. Why? Did you?"

"Yeah."

"No way!" She yells this out like it's pretty funny that I'd get sick.

"*Way!*" I yell back.

"But you barely had anything to drink."

I shrug. "To be honest, I lost count."

"As I recall, *you* were the one who was all sobered up after falling into the pool." This makes her laugh. "I can still see you standing there, dripping wet and looking like someone had pulled a fast one. Did your sweatshirt recover?"

I frown. "I'm not sure. I think it's still in the backseat."

She glances over her shoulder. "Yuck. That's gonna smell if you don't get it outta here."

"So, seriously, you never got sick?"

"No. I just went to bed and fell asleep."

"Man, I was hugging John for about an hour I think."

"Hugging John?"

"You know, the toilet. He and I are on a first-name basis now."

She's laughing really hard now. "Hey, don't feel bad. I've been there and done that."

"But how can you drink as much as you do and not get sick?" I demand as I turn down the street to the high school.

"Guess my body's used to it. No biggie."

I consider this as we drive down the street in silence. Finally I say, "But it can't be very good for you, can it?"

"It's not as dangerous as drugs."

"Yeah, well, it's not as dangerous as BASE jumping either."

"Why are you so grumpy this morning?" she demands as I pull into the student parking lot.

"I don't know. I guess I'm just thinking I shouldn't be drinking so much."

"Well, then don't."

I nod as I turn into an available parking space. "Okay, I won't."

"But can we still be friends?" Her voice sounds small and far away, and suddenly I feel like I must've been a little harsh, like I'm blaming her for my own stupid choices.

"Of course we can be friends."

She smiles. "Good, because I wanted to take you to lunch today."

"You mean in the cafeteria?"

"No, silly. There's a new deli on High Street. I want to go there."

"But we have closed campus. The parking lot is locked."

"The deli is only three blocks away. We'll walk. Kids go off campus all the time, Amber. It's no big deal. They just don't like you driving cars around. Come on, are you in? It's my treat."

Being taken out to lunch does sound like a good deal. And besides, Claire seems to really need me as a friend, and, I assure myself, a lunch date at a public restaurant can't possibly involve drinking—well, unless she's got her flask on her. But I can't imagine her being bold enough to bring it to school. She'd be in serious trouble if she got caught. "Okay," I finally say as we cross the street in front of the school. "Lunch sounds great."

"Cool. Meet me by the west door near the gym." She pauses before we part ways. "Thanks for being such a good friend, Amber. I really appreciate it."

I see Simi's little orange Volkswagen Bug turn in to the parking lot now, and I wave. She waves back but looks a little curious when she notices I'm with Claire. Oh, well. I tell Claire I'll see her later and then decide to wait in front of the school for Simi.

"How's it going?" Simi asks as she joins me. "Have you saved her yet?"

Now, I find lame comments like this seriously irksome. "You know that it's not up to us to save someone," I say in irritation. "Only God can do that."

"Yeah, yeah," she says. "I'm just jerking your chain. Like, what do you expect when you're playing barroom evangelism?"

"Barroom evangelism?"

"That's what Pastor Glen calls it, and he says it doesn't work."

"How did he figure that out?"

"In college. He said he tried to witness to people in bars before, but it usually backfired on him."

"Maybe he wasn't doing it right."

"The problem was, he ended up drinking too and ended up looking like a total fool—not that you'd know anything about that."

We're going into the school now, and I really don't want to continue this conversation. "Can we talk about something else?" I ask.

So Simi tells me about how Lena has taken over the bonus room above her parents' garage. "I thought the place was just a nasty rattrap," says Simi, "but you should see how cool it looks now. Lena fixed it all up."

I make the appropriate comments, and then the bell rings and we part ways. "See you at lunch," she calls as she hurries toward the art department.

I never have a chance to say that I won't see her at lunch, but maybe it doesn't matter. She'd probably just worry anyway. And it's not like we eat lunch together every day—okay, *almost* every day. But maybe it's time for a change.

I go back and forth all morning. Sometimes I tell myself that I need to bail on the lunch thing with Claire, and other times I wonder why I'm so freaked about it—and everything else. Why can't I just relax and lighten up? Sheesh, maybe I *do* need a drink.

Anyway, it's finally lunchtime, and I'm walking by the gym when I hear Claire calling my name. I join her, and when no one's looking, we duck out the side door and head across the soccer field toward the street. It's one of the few parts of our school that still hasn't been fenced in yet, although I'm sure it's just a matter of time. Honestly, I think someday they'll have electric fences and guard dogs. I'm not sure if it'll be to keep kids in or out, but it's not fun feeling like you're penned up in a prison camp.

"This is great," I admit to Claire as we walk like freed people, breathing the air and feeling the sunshine. "I should do this more often."

"That's what I'm telling you." She points to other kids who have escaped the confines of school. "See, everyone does it."

I don't mention that it looks like some of them have gone out for a smoke or that I'm a little concerned about the shape of the cigarettes that some of them are smoking. It's no secret that a lot of kids at our school smoke weed. I just don't happen to know any of them personally. In most ways, I suppose I've led a pretty sheltered life. And this recent thing with drinking and partying is something of an eye-opener, although I don't want to admit that. I want to be cool with all this. I mean, I'm eighteen—isn't it time for me to grow up?

It takes about five minutes to get to the deli, and I have to admit that it looks like a great little place, with blue canvas awnings and outdoor seating, like something right out of Europe—not that I've been there. The place is called Merenda's, and when we go inside, there is jazz music playing, and suddenly I feel very grown-up.

I study the handwritten menu on the easel near the counter to discover this place is a giant step up from the boring selection of food in the cafeteria, but not feeling overly adventuresome, I finally decide on the corned beef sandwich. Claire orders pumpkin soup and salad and then—just as calm as can be—orders a glass of wine (a Pinot Noir, whatever that is). Well, I try not to look totally shocked, but I'm feeling pretty curious as to what this cashier is going to do. Without being obvious, I glance at Claire, and although she could probably pass for twenty-one (especially when, like today, she's dressed so stylishly), I also know the law. Cashiers are supposed to card anyone who looks less than thirty. I watch and wait.

"May I see your ID?" asks the older woman.

"Sure," says Claire, reaching into her purse for her wallet. "I'm used to being carded," she tells her in an offhanded way. "My mom says the sad thing is when you don't get carded anymore. But then, she's in her forties."

The woman laughs and hands back the driver's license. "I know how your mom feels," she says sadly. "I can't even remember the last time I was carded."

And that's it. We take our number and go sit down at a corner table and wait for our order. But when I'm sure that the woman is safely out of hearing distance, I ask Claire about her ID. "Where did you get that?"

"Well, it's fake, of course. But I know a guy who's really good at this. I'm not sure how he does it, but his IDs never get questioned."

"Can I see it?"

"Not here," she says, smiling up at the woman who is now bringing our lunches, along with Claire's glass of red wine.

"Anything else?" asks the woman.

"No, thanks. This looks perfect," says Claire.

Before we leave, Claire has the nerve to order another glass of wine! And then, after leaving a generous tip for the oblivious woman, Claire drinks it up and we leave. I'm sure my hands are shaking as we exit Merenda's. I don't even know why. I mean, it's not as if I've done anything wrong, but I'm finding that Claire's nerve is very unnerving.

Claire laughs as we walk back to school. "Lighten up, Amber. It's no big deal. Did you know that kids in France drink wine all the time? I went there with Mom and Mike a couple summers ago, right after they got married. I was only sixteen, and I got to drink wine whenever I wanted to."

"Seriously?" I find this hard to believe. "Your mom let you drink wine in France?"

"*Oui, mademoiselle.* And she even used to let me drink it at home too—not a lot, but for special dinners and holidays and stuff. Unfortunately, she's changed her thinking on that whole thing, as well as a bunch of other things too. That's why I've taken matters into my own hands lately." Then she pops a breath mint into her mouth. "Want one?"

I nod and silently accept a mint.

"Now, what we need to do is get you a fake ID, Amber. It's really easy. All I need is your photo, like one from last year's yearbook. That's where I got mine."

"I don't know . . ." I say. "For one thing, my junior picture does *not* look like I'm twenty-one. But besides that, it just doesn't seem right."

"Oh, come on, Amber. It's no big deal. I want to do this for you. Why don't you just let me take care of it and you can see what you think when it's finished?"

Just then we are joined by a couple of girls. They are coming back to school after eating at Benny's Burger Joint. And when Claire tells them about our lunch at Merenda's, they are quite impressed. They're all friends of Claire's—or at least they used to be. But to my surprise, they are quite nice and actually seem to like Claire and care about her. We tell them about our lunch, and Claire even admits to using a fake ID to buy wine.

"No way," says Haley. "You got away with that in broad daylight?"

Claire nods proudly.

"How about you?" Megan asks me.

I shake my head. "I don't have a fake ID."

"Not yet," says Claire, "but she will."

Soon they are all pulling out their fake IDs and showing me. It's like these small plastic cards are some kind of badge of courage or medal of honor or ticket to freedom, and it's not long before I think it might actually be cool to have a fake ID too.

"It can get you into some really good clubs," says Haley. "And you can meet new people and hear some pretty cool bands play."

"Just don't overdo the drinking part," warns Megan. "Don't follow Claire's bad example."

"Give me a break," says Claire with a hurt expression. "Haven't you heard? I've been doing better lately."

"Really?" Megan's raised brows and firm mouth look somewhat unconvinced.

"Yes," says Claire with an air of confidence. "Amber's a good influence on me."

Now Megan is smiling at me as though this being a good influence is really a good thing. And I think I actually feel a small flutter of pride, like maybe I really am helping Claire after all, like maybe God is at work here. But at the same time, I wonder how that can possibly be true.

Megan and Claire are walking together ahead of me now, and Megan is expressing her sympathy over Claire's breakup with Tommy. I listen from behind and feel, I hate to admit, just a little bit jealous, like that maybe I'll be left behind now that Megan is back in the picture.

Just then, Haley turns around. "Don't worry," she says in this unexpected confidential tone. "Those two don't have a real chance of becoming good friends again." Then she really lowers her voice and tells me that Megan has already moved in on Tommy and is simply trying to make things okay with Claire first. Well, I don't even know how to respond to that, and so I don't. But I do think the way these girls operate is rather mysterious. But then I've always felt that way about popularity in general.

I guess the most amazing thing is that I'm here right now, right in their midst, as if I'm really part of their group. And even stranger is the fact that they seem to be, for the most part, accepting me. Of course, I know this is only because of Claire. And her acceptance among her peers seems to be somewhat shaky, to say the least. Still, I'm thinking this whole thing is kind of fun—while it lasts anyway. The more I'm around Claire and her drinking habits, the more comfortable I'm getting with the whole thing. Like really, what's the big deal anyway?

eight

Simi meets up with me at my locker, but I can't quite read her expression.

"I know, I know," I say to her, hoping to cut right to the chase. "You're probably wondering where I was at lunch. I would've told you, but I didn't see you around. Claire invited me to have lunch with her and—"

"Did you guys drink?"

I give her my best offended look. "No, officer," I say indignantly. "Do you want to smell my breath or make me walk a line?"

She shakes her head. "Well, you can't blame me for thinking that—not after the past few days."

I nod and attempt to look somewhat contrite. "I know. But if it makes you feel any better, Claire actually told her other friends that I'm a good influence on her. And they seemed to be relieved. So there."

"Really?"

"Yeah. Maybe God really is at work here, Simi." I feel sort of excited now, like I'm actually believing this myself. "I mean, he does work in mysterious ways. Maybe he's going to use me to get through to those girls."

Simi nods. "Yeah, you could be right. I guess really I should be praying for them. Wouldn't it be cool if God did something big at our school before graduation?"

"Maybe that's what's happening."

We talk about this some more as we walk to class together, and she seems both surprised and impressed when Haley and Stacy wave at us, like maybe she's really convinced.

"Oh, yeah," she says as we're about to part ways, "my aunt said to stop by after school. I told her you get out early, and she said around two would be great."

"Thanks," I tell her. "When do you start?"

"Tomorrow."

After fifth period, I find Claire and explain that I won't be around to give her a ride home like I'd planned.

"You're so lucky to have early release. I should've worked harder last year."

"Well, at least you don't have to get a part-time job to earn money," I remind her. "I think I'd rather be in school than working in some silly candy store."

"Well, just don't start eating that stuff," she warns. "You could be a porker by graduation time."

I roll my eyes. "Thanks for the encouragement."

"Oh, yeah," she says suddenly, lowering her voice and looking around. "I heard that Slater Ross thinks you're pretty cool. I think he's going to ask you out."

"No way," I say in a hushed voice. "Who told you that?"

"Haley. She and Slater are friends—just friends. Not only that, but Haley thinks you're cool too."

"Seriously?"

"Yeah. I think everyone used to think you were just a Little Miss

Perfect. Now that you're lightening up, they're seeing you in a whole new light."

I nod. "Cool."

"Let me know if anything happens with Slater."

"For sure."

"You guys would be a good couple. Maybe he'll ask you to the prom." Now she gets a sad expression. "But I guess I'll be home alone that night."

I reach out and put my hand on her arm. "Hey, the prom isn't such a big deal."

She shrugs. "Well, I've probably been to more than my fair share already. And don't worry, I've already heard about Megan making the move on Tommy. I don't really care. She can have him if she wants him that bad."

"Really? You're okay with it?"

"There are other fish in the sea." Then she laughs. "I sound just like my mom!"

I laugh. "Well, it may be corny, but it's true."

"In fact . . ." She looks as if she just thought of something. "There's this guy I met a couple weeks ago. He doesn't go to our school. Hmmm . . ."

I slap her on the back. "Okay, you go, girl."

"Maybe we can double-date to the prom."

"Yeah, sure. I don't even have a date."

Claire wriggles her eyebrows. "We'll see."

"Well, I better go. I'm supposed to have an interview around two and I think I should go home and change first."

"For The Caramel Corn Shoppe?" She shakes her head. "I think you look just fine. But I better go. I'm late for class."

We take off in different directions. Now, while I'm slightly relieved not to be giving Claire a ride home today, I also feel disappointed to leave her. I mean, she really can be such fun. And all this talk about Slater and the prom, well, it's pretty exciting stuff—at least for me. I've never even gone to the prom. I never actually thought I ever would. Now, Simi has a chance to go since this guy in her art class has asked her like a million times, but she keeps putting him off. Maybe if she thought I were going she'd go.

Anyway, I have to push these thoughts from my head as I do my little interview with Simi's aunt. Jan is a lot younger than Simi's mom. Probably in her early thirties, I'm guessing. She's not married and although she's pretty, she's a little on the pudgy side, which is probably understandable when you realize she owns The Caramel Corn Shoppe. But she seems like a genuinely nice person and, although she's not a Christian, she appreciates the fact that my dad is a pastor.

"So you probably need to have Sundays off," she says like I already have the job.

"Well, I noticed your sign says you don't open until noon. If I go to early service, I could easily be here by that time."

She brightens. "And what about Saturday nights?" she asks. "Simi said you guys have youth group that night."

I consider this. "Well, that's true. But I've gone to church and youth group my whole life. I don't think it'd hurt to miss a few." Her sign also says that the shop closes at seven thirty on Saturdays, and I figure that might still give me time to have a little fun, not to mention a good excuse to miss youth group—not that I'm really planning to do that. I mean, that would be wrong.

"Well, if you want the job, it's yours, Amber. I will be so relieved to finally have some responsible girls in here."

I smile. "And you don't have to worry about me eating the

merchandise," I assure her. "I don't have that much of a sweet tooth and I'm trying to watch my weight." Oops, I wish I hadn't said that—she might take it personally.

But she just laughs. "You and me both. But let me warn you, this place can be pretty tempting sometimes."

"I don't know." I glance around the colorful shop as I consider this. "I think just the smell of all this sugar might make me think I don't want any."

"Well, I have this little trick," she admits. "I let my workers eat as much of anything and everything they want during their first day on the job. Usually they get sick and for the most part avoid sneaking treats after that—although the girl I just fired liked to give stuff away to all her friends." Jan makes an angry face that I think might be a warning. *"That really burns me."*

"Yeah, I can imagine. Well, don't worry about that with me. My parents have raised me to know the difference between right and wrong."

"Good for them."

But now I'm wondering how much truth was in that last claim. I mean, sure, I *know* the difference between right and wrong, but I haven't exactly been choosing too carefully lately. Still, that might all be changing now—or at least that's what I tell myself.

"So when can you start?" she's asking me.

"Uh, anytime."

"Well, Simi is starting tomorrow. Since I have to train her, why don't I train you at the same time? We'll kill two birds with one stone."

So it's agreed and she hands me some papers and tells me to come in tomorrow at three. "You guys can do the three-to-nine shift. We're open until nine on every day except Saturday and Sunday."

"I saw the sign," I remind her.

"Oh, yeah. Okay, see you tomorrow."

My parents seem surprisingly happy to hear I've taken a part-time job. I'm not sure what's up with that, but I guess they're assuming my earnings will all go into my savings account for college. And while some of it will, I plan to have a little fun too. Like Claire says, this is the end of our senior year and we should make it something we never forget.

"Did you get the job?" asks Simi when she calls shortly after dinner.

"Yep," I tell her. "Jan is going to train both of us tomorrow."

"Cool." I can hear relief in her voice. "Now maybe things will get back to normal again."

"Normal?"

She laughs. "Oh, you know. With us and the way we both are trying to follow God and be good Christian examples. You know what I mean."

"Oh, yeah." I notice the flatness in my voice. "I guess that's normal."

"Hey, did you hear there's going to be a citywide evangelism thing this summer? I can't remember what it's called, but Lena was telling me about it yesterday. They're trying to get volunteers from all the different churches in town to help with counseling and stuff. I'm surprised your dad hasn't mentioned it."

"Actually, he was just talking about it at dinner." I try to sound more enthused than I feel. "It's called Stand Up! and it's some kind of crusade. I guess our church is going to get involved too."

"Sounds cool. Maybe we can get some kids from school to come. I hear they're going to have some Christian bands and speakers directed at our age group."

"That'll be great."

"Well, I hope we'll have time to be involved—I mean, now that we've got jobs and stuff."

"Hey, even though I'm working, I still plan on having a life," I tell her.

"Duh."

We talk some more about Stand Up! and finally I tell her that I really have to get to my homework. "I kind of neglected it this weekend."

"Yeah, I'm sure you did."

But the truth is, I just want to get off the phone. All this talk about evangelism makes me feel uncomfortable or maybe guilty. I mean, how can I be involved in something like that when I'm not even praying these days? In some ways it feels like I've turned my back on God completely. I try to convince myself that I'm on vacation, like I've worked so hard and for so long being a good Christian that I deserve a break. And maybe I do.

My cell phone rings again, and this time it's Claire. "What's up?" I ask.

"The best news!" she gushes. "I talked to Slater today, and he *does* like you. He said he looked for you at lunch today but couldn't find you." She laughs. "I told him that was my fault, but he was totally impressed when he heard what we'd done."

"You're kidding!" I say as I crash onto my bed. "That is so cool."

"Yeah. And we were talking about how to get you guys together, and he thought maybe he could take you out for coffee." She laughs. "Yeah, that sounds like fun."

"Hey, it sounds fine to me."

"Well, maybe for starters. Anyway, I think he's going to talk to you tomorrow, so you better make yourself available."

"Cool."

We talk some more, but I notice that Claire seems to have a hard time staying with me in the conversation, like maybe she's watching TV or something. Then it occurs to me that her words are slightly slurred.

"Have you been drinking?" I ask.

"Huh?"

"I'm just curious," I say, hoping that I'm not sounding all confrontational or anything. "Have you had something to drink?"

"Oh, yeah, just a couple. No big deal."

I want to ask her why she drinks so much and whether she's concerned about her health and stuff, but it's like I can't find the words. "Well, I better go," I finally say. "I've still got homework."

"Homework . . ." Her voice kind of trails off.

"Yeah. Take care, okay?"

"Yeah, sure." Then she hangs up and I feel bad, like maybe I offended her. However, I doubt she'll even remember it tomorrow.

So after I finish up my homework, I decide to do a little research. Now, I'm sure Claire and her friends would think this is totally ridiculous, not to mention nerdy, but this is just the way I normally think. I like to get the facts. Maybe I am a nerd. But since my computer's on, I decide to start Googling information about alcohol.

Okay, I have to admit that most of what I'm reading is pretty scary stuff. But it seems that the worst danger lies with binge drinking. That means consuming more alcohol than your body can handle. I don't think that's what I'm into—at least I hope not. And I'll try to make sure I avoid that. I've also learned that if you eat food and drink water, you should be okay with just a couple of drinks.

Okay, maybe I am whitewashing this a bit, since I keep avoiding the sites that seem to be filled with gloom and doom. I mean, I want to be realistic about the dangers, but no need to go off the deep end, right? I mean, like one of the statistics I read is that next to caffeine, alcohol is the most widely used drug in the world. But then, who really considers caffeine to be a drug or dangerous? I also read that moderate use (like one glass of wine) is actually good for cholesterol levels—not that I need to worry about that.

Finally I am too sleepy to focus my eyes and so I turn off the computer and try not to obsess over the various ways alcohol can affect a person. I'll think about that tomorrow.

nine

I PUT ON WHAT I THINK IS A FAIRLY COOL OUTFIT AND TRY TO "MAKE myself available" the next day, but I only see Slater once, and he seems totally oblivious to me. Not only that, but Claire also seems to be avoiding me. Of course, Simi is around, and that's some consolation, but for some reason, I feel like I'm being blown off by everyone else. And sitting with Simi Gartolini and Lisa Chan during lunch is—how can I put this politely?—*boring*.

"It's nice to have you back," says Lisa. "I thought maybe you'd gone over to the dark side."

"The dark side?" I stare at her like she's an alien.

She laughs. "I'm just kidding. But seriously, Simi told me about how you've been drinking and—"

"Simi *told* you?" I turn to stare at Simi now.

"I just asked her to be praying for you—"

"I don't need people praying for me, thank you very much."

"Well, we've been concerned," says Lisa defensively. "And it's just because we love you and want—"

"Maybe you should try loving some other people," I suggest as I finish off the last bite of my burger. "Like people who don't go to church or call themselves Christians." Then I stand up.

"Oh, don't get all mad, Amber."

I smile at them in the way I've been trained to for years. "I'm not mad at you guys. I just need to stop by the library before fifth period. See you later."

But the truth is, I'm seething as I dump my tray and head for the exit. But I'm not just mad at Lisa and Simi—I'm also really frustrated at Claire and Slater. I feel like they've let me down. I mean, why is everyone suddenly treating me like I'm some kind of social disease? I stop by the bathroom and look in the mirror. Is something wrong with me? Like, do I have spinach in my teeth or a big red zit on my chin or a booger in my nose? Is there something I've failed to notice that's driving people away? But all I see is the sad face of a preacher's kid who doesn't quite know where she fits in anymore.

"Get over yourself," I whisper to my image. "Everything is not about you." Okay, it sounds good, but I don't really believe it. I head off to my last class feeling like the loser that I am, and it's no big surprise when nobody notices or talks to me. I am so relieved when class is over and it's time to go to work.

Simi and I have already decided to take separate cars since it's just easier, and I leave school so quickly that I'm pretty sure I'll get there before her. Besides, I have to change into my work clothes, which are actually just black pants and a white T-shirt but are what Jan has instructed us to wear. Naturally, I refuse to do this changing at school since I'd be too embarrassed to be seen walking around in such a boring sort of preppy outfit. Of course, Simi says it's no big deal and that she plans to change in the girls' bathroom. I plan to change at the public restroom in the mall.

It's not even three o'clock when I show up at The Caramel Corn Shoppe all dressed and ready to go. I gave myself a little pep talk as I tied my hair back into a ponytail, and I am now determined to put my disappointing day behind me and be the best employee Jan has ever hired.

"You're early," she says with a smile. "I like that."

"Simi should be here soon."

Then she hands me the dreaded uniform, which is really a red-and-white gingham apron. It has a bib that's got a ruffle around it and looks like something out of the last millennium. "I expect you to wear this at all times when you're at work," she says in a firm voice. "My customers expect it, and it's like our assurance of quality and cleanliness." Then she proceeds to lecture me about hygiene and how important it is to wash my hands regularly.

I nod and listen as if I'm very impressed with this technical level of training, and then Simi shows up and I am subjected to the same lecture all over again.

After Simi and I demonstrate that we both already know how to use a cash register and that we are capable of following the very specific and rather simple directions on the caramel-corn machine, Jan decides to leave us on our own for a bit while she makes a coffee run.

"This looks pretty easy," I say as soon as Jan is out the door.

"Yeah, and it's never very busy in here on weekdays."

"In other words, it's probably going to be pretty boring."

She shrugs.

"I wonder why she needs both of us here at once."

"I think it's just until she's convinced we're trained."

Then our first customers come in. It's a mom with two young children who, in my opinion, may be more in need of a nap than a sugar high. But after several squabbles and a few tears, they all finally agree to a quarter pound of jelly beans and a medium box of caramel corn. I weigh and bag the jelly beans while Simi fills the box. Then I let Simi (since she's Jan's niece) do the cash register. And when I glance at the clock, I'm dismayed to see that it's only three thirty. At this rate, I'll be a hundred years old by closing time.

I stifle a big yawn and reach for the Windex. Jan made it clear that we are to stay busy when there are no customers, and it looks like the glass on the candy counter could use a cleaning.

"Good girl," says Jan when she returns with her coffee.

And so goes the afternoon. Boring, boring, boring. But hey, at least I'm making money, right?

Simi and I are both hugely relieved when Jan leaves us to take a dinner break.

"How does she make any money off this place?" I ask Simi. "I mean, so far we couldn't have sold more than twenty dollars worth of stuff. That can't possibly even cover our wages."

Simi shrugs. "My mom says that Grandma Gartolini left Jan most of her money."

"More than your dad got?"

"I don't know. He doesn't talk about it, but I think Jan must've been the favorite, since she was the baby. And maybe my grandma thought my dad was doing okay since he had his law practice and everything. But Aunt Jan was kind of just floundering around."

"And she spent her inheritance on this shop?"

Simi laughs now. "Dad always says that his baby sister was absent on the day that the brains were handed out." Then she gets serious. "Customer alert," she says in a stern voice.

I turn around to see that not only is this a "customer alert" but it's also a "kids from our school alert," and I suddenly wish I could disappear or maybe make a quick trip to the back room.

"Hey, there," says Slater with a smile.

"Hey," I say, pasting on my Sunday smile. "How's it going?"

"Okay."

Kent Fischer is with Slater, which makes this unexpected meeting even more awkward. "You really work here?" says Kent. The last time I spoke to him was at his little get-together on Saturday night, and I'm sure I seemed like a different person then.

I can feel my face flushing as I nod. "Yeah, I just started." I gesture toward Simi. "Simi's aunt owns the shop and we both just started today." Okay, I know I sound totally lame. Why am I babbling on like this, like I think they even care? And what are they doing here anyway? I wish I could just disappear.

"You guys want some caramel corn or something?" asks Simi as if she's not talking to a couple of the coolest guys in school. And I have to wonder what makes her so grounded and secure. Is it just because she's beautiful? And if so, how is that fair?

I notice that Kent is really studying her now, looking at her like he's never even seen her before. "Nice outfits," he says in a teasing voice.

She calmly smiles. "Thanks. I feel like a real domestic goddess in this little number."

He laughs. "Okay, I guess I'll have some caramel corn after all." He studies the sizes of boxes on the display. "How about a large?"

"No problem."

As Simi takes care of Kent's order, Slater seems to be focusing on me. "I was looking for you at school today," he says quietly.

I feel my brows rising in that "yeah, sure" expression, but "oh" is all I can come up with. Clever.

"Did Claire tell you anything?" he continues.

Suddenly I'm realizing that Slater might be on the shy side, although this has never occurred to me before. I mean, he hangs with the cool kids and likes to party and stuff. "Yeah," I say quickly.

"Claire did mention something." But that's all he's getting from me. I am not about to bring up the subject of going out for coffee.

"Well, do you get a break or anything tonight?" he asks.

I feel my heart sinking. "I actually had my break already," I admit.

"Oh. Well, I just got out of track practice and thought I'd stop in and say hey."

I smile now. "I'm glad you did."

He turns away from me and looks at the caramel-corn boxes now. "I guess I'll take a small box of that stuff."

"That *stuff*?" I sort of tease. "Haven't you ever had caramel corn before?"

He looks slightly embarrassed now. "Actually, I haven't."

"Oh." So I turn around and make myself busy by filling a small box as full as I can get it. I fill it and shake it down and then fill it again, knowing I'm taking way too long and probably looking like a total nerd. Why does something this simple have to feel so awkward? I remember how easily we talked at Kent's house on Saturday night. Why is it so hard now?

I give him the box, and he hands me a five-dollar bill. I push the buttons on the cash register and then count out his change, noticing the sparks I get when my hand touches his. Can he feel it too?

"Maybe tomorrow night?" he says as I give him the last quarter.

"Huh?"

"For coffee?"

I nod. "Yeah, sure. That would be great."

"So do you work tomorrow too?"

"Yeah, but I could save my break for when you get here."

He smiles now. "Cool."

Then Kent makes a few more comments about our charming outfits and the shop in general, and then they take their caramel corn and leave. I can't believe how relieved I am once they're gone, and yet at the same time, I wish they'd stayed longer. Confusing.

"I think I forgot to wear deodorant today," I tell Simi as I check my pits, which makes her laugh.

"Are you really that nervous?"

"Yeah." I look at her like *duh.*

"Do you really like him that much?"

"Could you tell?"

She rolls her eyes.

"It looked like Kent was really checking you out," I say, hoping this will change the subject.

She shrugs. "He's not my type. Besides, doesn't he go with Haley Banks?"

"I guess."

"So you have it bad for Slater Ross," she says.

"I never said that."

"You don't need to."

"I barely know him."

"But you'd like to get to know him better?"

"Yeah, why not?"

"Is he a Christian?"

"I don't know."

"Maybe you should find out."

I reaffix my Sunday smile to my face. "Maybe I will. We're going to have coffee during my break tomorrow."

"You don't even drink coffee."

I smile again. "I do now."

Then she tosses a wadded-up paper towel at me and just groans as though I'm making the worst mistake of my life.

"Simi," I say, trying to be honest and sincere. "I'm not saying I have all the answers here, but I just don't see how it's wrong to spend time with someone who doesn't happen to be saved. I mean, how are people ever going to get saved if we're always pushing them away?"

"Now, are we talking about dating evangelism?" she asks with one arched brow.

"I don't know." I throw up my hands. "Do we have to label everything?"

She shrugs. "Maybe not."

Then Jan returns from her dinner break, and a few more customers start trickling in. To my relief, the next two hours pass a little more quickly. Jan teaches us how to shut down and clean out the equipment, and suddenly it's quitting time.

"You girls did a good job tonight," she says. "How about if you both come again tomorrow, and then I'll make up a schedule?"

The three of us walk outside together, and I can't help but wonder if there isn't this smell of sugar wafting all around us. I'm surprised that the security guard doesn't actually stop and sniff as we pass by.

Later that night, as I'm doing homework on the computer, I get an instant message from Claire.

sorry i waz mess today. u ok?

Curious as to what this is about, I write back.

what do u mean? how r u a mess?

drank 2 much. got sik. not there 4 u.

that's ok. how r u now?

feel like crud. maybe i drink 2 much. ya think?

Okay, I'm not sure how to react to this. It's the first time I've ever heard her question herself. Usually she's just defensive. I don't know what to say.

what do u think?

don't know. but tired of letting people down. don't wanna be a loser. u know? all my friends say i let them down. everyone says i drink 2 much. what do u think?

Okay, this seems like an opportunity here, but I'm just not sure what to say. I mean, it's not like I'm a counselor or anything.

maybe u should talk 2 professional?

a shrink?

don't know. but i read about alcohol online and found some scary stuff

are u preaching 2 me?

no! just care about u. concerned 4 ur health. u know?

yeah, maybe ur rite. maybe i do need help.

can't hurt 2 talk 2 someone. my church has counselor. she's free and pretty nice. no one would know.

i'll think about it. thx. u r good friend.

take care of urself. ok?

ok

Now, I know this is just a small thing, but I'm thinking, *See, God might be at work here. Who knows?*

ten

I GUESS I SHOULD BE THANKFUL THAT MY BREAK IS ONLY TWENTY MINUTES long, because on Wednesday night, the following night, there are these long awkward silences between Slater and me.

"How was track practice?" I ask, struggling to find something—anything—to get this conversation going.

"Hard."

"Are you looking forward to Friday's meet?"

"Not really."

Okay, I'm thinking, *help me out here, Slater.*

"How's work going?" he asks.

"Boring."

He smiles. "Yeah, it seems a little slow in there."

"Jan says it's better on weekends."

"You have to work on weekends?"

I nod. "But at least the store closes early, so my evenings are free." Okay, now, does that sound like a hint or what? How stupid can I be anyway?

"What about Friday?" he asks.

I swallow the sip of bitter coffee and wonder if I'll get used to this stuff. "Friday?" I echo, wondering if maybe he really is asking me out.

"Yeah, you said you might come to the meet. Are you still going to do that?"

I nod, remembering how I said I wanted to see him run. "I'll have to check the schedule and see."

He smiles and looks at his watch.

"Yeah," I say. "I think my break is just about up."

He walks me back to The Caramel Corn Shoppe, and I feel certain that this, our first "date," is a total failure.

"See you," he says.

"Thanks for the coffee," I say, feeling lamer than ever. I mean, what is wrong with me that I can't carry on a more interesting conversation? It's like I'm socially constipated. Is that possible?

Fortunately, Jan is there and Simi is keeping up the appearance of being busy and doesn't have a chance to quiz me about my little coffee date. But when Jan takes her break, Simi comes at me full force.

"Don't worry," I finally tell her. "I was so totally boring that I'm absolutely certain he will never ask me out again. In fact, I'm sure he was hugely relieved that he'd only asked me out for coffee and that I only had twenty minutes. I mean, what if it had been a whole evening? What a disaster."

She smiles as if this is just the kind of answer she had hoped for. In fact, she was probably praying that the whole thing would go south on me. "Well, don't feel bad, Amber. It's probably for the best anyway."

Now, that just totally steams me. I mean, how does *she* know what's for the best? Argh!

"I made a schedule," announces Jan just as we're closing up. "It's on the bulletin board if you want to copy it."

Simi and I go over, and I am surprised to see that I have Friday off. I guess I could actually go to Slater's track meet now—that is, if I'm desiring a little more social torture. I'm not too sure about that at the moment.

"We both work on Saturday," says Simi with disappointment. "We'll miss youth group."

"We could always go late," I suggest.

Jan is standing looking over our shoulders now. "Or I could come in and close and let you leave early."

"You'd do that?"

"Well, not every Saturday, mind you," says Jan, "but once in a while. And especially if you're good workers. And if I don't have a date." She laughs. "As if *that's* a problem!"

"You should join the singles' group at our church," says Simi. "You might meet Mr. Right there."

This makes Jan laugh even harder. "Hey, if I were seriously looking for Mr. Right, that would be the last place I'd look."

As we walk out to the parking lot together, Simi continues to urge her aunt to try going to church, but Jan just keeps blowing her off. I want to tell Simi not to be so pushy, but then I figure she's talking to her own aunt. Surely she knows how much the poor woman can take.

I try not to obsess over the mess I made of my "date" with Slater tonight, but as soon as I get in my car, my cell phone is ringing, and it's Claire.

"How'd it go?" she asks.

"What?" I ask, although I'm sure that I know exactly what she's talking about.

"Slater."

I sigh. "It was pretty pathetic," I admit.

"Pathetic? Do you mean you or him?"

"Both, I think. Or maybe it was just me. I'm pretty boring."

"You guys should've gone out for drinks."

I laugh. "Yeah, that's a brilliant idea." I don't ask her about our instant-messaging chat last night because she already gave me the hint earlier today that she didn't want to talk about that just yet.

"Well, I think I'm going to give that boy a call."

"Oh, don't do that," I plead. "I mean, that is really desperate and I'll look like— "

"Trust me," she says. "I know just how to handle this."

"Whatever." I realize that I'm the only one in the parking lot now. "Hey, I better go," I say quickly. "I'm sitting by myself in the back parking lot of the mall, and I feel like a mugging that's about to happen."

"Well, get out of there!"

I am halfway home when my phone rings again.

"You won't believe this," she tells me in a breathless voice. "Slater is still really interested in you, but he confessed that he's really hopeless when it comes to starting a relationship, and he's happy to get any help."

"Seriously?"

"Yes, and so I told him that I'd heard an ad for Lola's on the radio and— "

"What's Lola's?"

"*What's Lola's?*" Her voice is incredulous. "What? Do you like live under a rock or something?"

"Sorry, but I've been kind of out of it."

She laughs. "Well, just don't go around saying something like that when real people are listening. Okay, Lola's happens to be the best club in Stanfield. Everyone who's anyone has been there. And they get a lot of up-and-coming bands. Like last fall, they had this indie band called Arnold that has gone huge recently. And this weekend they're having an underground British band called Distance-Walker that is supposed to be awesome."

"Uh, let me guess. I bet you need an ID card to get in."

"Well, yeah. But I think Alex could have yours ready by Saturday."

"Saturday?" I don't tell her that Saturday is youth-group night. I'm sure she wouldn't understand.

"Yeah. Is there a problem? I mean, Slater really wants to hear this band, and he'd like to go with you. He's going to ask you tomorrow, Amber. I'm just trying to give you a heads-up on it."

I suddenly imagine Slater and me at this really great club, listening to an underground British band (whatever that means), and it sounds pretty grown-up and exciting to me. "Okay," I tell her. "That sounds good. And if Slater actually asks me, I'm sure I'll say yes."

Claire makes a squealing noise that hurts my ears and almost makes me run a red light.

"All right!" she yells. "I'll make sure that Alex has your ID card ready. And by the way, do you think it'll be okay if I tag along? I mean, I'm hoping I'll see Eric at Lola's. That's the guy I told you about, remember? He goes to North Ashton High, but I see him at parties and stuff. If I hadn't been dating Tommy, I probably would've hooked up with Eric ages ago."

"Yeah, that's fine. I think it'd be great if you came along. Do you think Slater will mind?"

"No. In fact, I suggested that we could all go together. He knows Eric too and totally understood my little plan."

"Cool."

"Yeah."

Then I remember something. "Oh, I almost forgot. I have to work on Saturday."

"Well, then get out of it."

"Actually, I think I can get off early. Is six thirty okay?"

"Yeah, it'll be fine. Trust me, Amber, this is going to be totally awesome."

But after I hang up, I begin to feel very nervous and kind of agitated. I mean, what am I agreeing to here? And how do I think I can get away with something like this? Not that there's anything wrong with listening to a good band once in a while. But to use a fake ID and go somewhere I'm really not supposed to be? Well, it feels like my conscience is actually kicking in big-time right now.

I pull over in front of McDonald's and dial Claire's number. I've decided that the only thing to do is back out before it's too late. I'm determined to say *forget it*, and I think she will understand.

"I just really don't think I can do this," I tell her in my best no-nonsense voice. "I mean, it sounds fun, but I know it's wrong—at least for me. My parents would totally freak if they found out that I—"

"Just chill, Amber!" She pauses, and I wait. "Now, listen to me. You're making this into a much bigger deal than it is. Take a deep breath and just chill, okay?"

I try taking a deep breath, but I still feel like this is all wrong, like the sooner she understands how I feel, the better it will be for everyone concerned. "It's not working," I tell her. "I think I should just bow out right now before Slater actually asks me and it gets—"

"No," insists Claire. "You *need* to do this, Amber. You're eighteen years old—that's old enough to vote and old enough to go to war. And you are definitely old enough to go out with a few friends, to hear a band, and even to have a drink or two if you want. It's no biggie."

"Maybe not for you—"

"Okay, I know what you need."

"What?"

"Never mind. I'll meet you at your house."

"But I thought you weren't supposed to drive?"

"It's okay for emergencies."

"But this isn't an—"

"Yes, it is. Now just relax, okay? I'll be there in fifteen minutes."

I hang up my phone and try to figure out what just happened. It seems impossible to think that Claire will actually be at my house in fifteen minutes. I don't think she even knows where I live. Besides that, she doesn't have a valid license. Now I wonder if she hasn't been drinking again and simply *talking under the influence*. The idea of that almost makes me laugh. Even so, I hurry home. I quietly go inside as if everything is perfectly normal.

Within five minutes, I hear our doorbell ring. Before my parents can get there, I dash to get it and there is Claire, standing on my porch with a big grin on her face. "You probably thought I didn't even know where you lived."

I pull her into the house, hoping I can get her to my room before my parents—

"Oh, you're home, Amber," says my dad as he halfway emerges from his den. "Was someone at the door?"

"A friend of mine," I say quickly.

He steps out completely now and removes his reading glasses and looks expectantly at Claire.

"This is my dad, Pastor Conrad," I say, using his title out of habit but wishing I hadn't. "And this is my friend Claire Phillips."

He shakes her hand and smiles. "Pleasure to meet you."

"We're working on some homework together tonight," I say, instantly regretting the lie. I hate lying to my dad.

"Kind of late, isn't it?"

"Well, I had to work, you know. This was the only time we could—"

"Your daughter is so sweet to help me like this," Claire says quickly. "I'm hopeless at English lit, but Amber is a real genius."

He laughs. "A genius, eh?"

"As if," I say and then tug Claire toward my bedroom. "Let's get to it." Of course, we then meet my mom in the hallway. She has on her bathrobe and slippers and looks somewhat confused, so I'm forced to go through introductions and explanations all over again.

"Oh, I've been wanting to meet you," my mom says as she looks at Claire and smiles warmly. "I've heard good things about you."

"Thanks," says Claire. "It's nice to meet you too."

Finally we are safely behind the closed door to my bedroom, but I still don't know what to think about Claire's little stunt.

eleven

"I CAN'T BELIEVE YOU REALLY CAME," I TELL HER AS I SINK DOWN INTO my beanbag chair and attempt to calm my jangled nerves. I look up to see that Claire is now taking a little walking tour of my room, and I'm embarrassed. I mean, my house must look like the slums compared to where she lives. I try not to feel totally mortified, but I just can't help it. Not only that, but I'm still wearing my lame work outfit. Talk about humiliating.

"Welcome to my humble abode," I finally mumble. "Not quite what you're used to, is it?"

"Very interesting décor," she finally says and then giggles. "What's up with these colors? Lime green, magenta, tangerine—looks like you couldn't make up your mind. Or maybe you were wasting away in margaritaville?"

"Yeah, that must've been it." Then, despite myself, I chuckle. "Okay, the truth is, I painted the place myself. I was about fifteen at the time and actually thought all these stripes of color would be cool. I'd seen one of those *Trading Spaces* episodes and thought, hey, how hard can it be?"

"Those shows crack me up," she says. "But don't you know that you're not supposed to attempt this at home?"

"Yeah, somehow the results weren't anything like on the TV show."

"I think it's actually kind of interesting," she says as she sits on my bed. My bedspread is actually a large piece of batik cloth that I found at a flea market. "Kind of seventies retro," she says. "Playful but serious."

Okay, now that makes me laugh. "Yeah, kind of like me, huh?"

"Yes. So are you over your crisis yet?"

"Crisis?"

"You know. It sounded like you were having a full-blown panic attack in the car."

I sigh. "Maybe just a conscience attack," I confess. "But seriously, won't you get in trouble for driving? I thought your license was suspended."

"Mom and Mike had to go to a business dinner that will probably go until really late. I borrowed my mom's wheels, and if she finds out, well, I'll simply tell her that you were a friend in need. She's really into loyalty. I think she'll understand."

"I don't know . . ."

Claire opens her bag and takes out a pink thermos and a couple of paper cups. "I brought over a little something to calm your nerves. And then we can talk."

I feel my eyes growing wide. I mean, I'm thinking, *Yeah, right, let's just get snookered right here in my bedroom so that my parents can walk in and have a freaking fit.* But she's already poured whatever this concoction is into a cup and is handing it to me.

"Come on," she says. "I made a special effort to come over here. The least you can do is have a drink."

And so despite all my fear and anxiety, I take a sip. And then I take another. And it's not long until I think I know exactly what she's talking about. It's like my troubles just start to melt away, and before you know it, I'm feeling more confident and happy. All of a sudden

I'm thinking, *Hey, what's the problem?*

We talk and laugh, and not once do my parents come bursting into my room to see whether we are drinking or not. Why would they? I've never given them a single reason not to trust me. Why would they stop trusting me now?

And when I realize it's getting pretty late and I attempt to quietly walk Claire (who's looking a bit unsteady) to her car, they still do not make an appearance. Once again, why should they?

"Drive carefully," I warn her, suddenly feeling some concern for her welfare.

"No problem," she assures me. "I have a special route to get home. No cops along there."

"Thanks for the pep talk," I say and then giggle. It's amazing that I really do feel better about everything now.

"So, it's settled then? You'll be going with us on Saturday?"

I nod. "Yeah, sounds like fun."

"Can I get a ride with you in the morning?"

"Sure. But don't forget I have to work afterward."

"Oh, yeah, the Caramel Corn Queen. Do you have to wear one of those aprons and everything?"

"Don't remind me."

She laughs and climbs into her mom's immaculate silver Mercedes and then smoothes her hair before putting in the key. Maybe she isn't as intoxicated as I think.

"Really," I remind her anyway. "Drive carefully, okay?"

She nods and then casually waves as she pulls straight out into the street without even glancing over her shoulder to make sure no one's coming. Fortunately, the street is empty.

Even so, I feel a little freaked as I watch her drive away, and I actually mutter a quick prayer for her safety. Then I slip back into the house and flop down on my bed and fall soundly asleep.

It's three in the morning when I wake up, and it feels like I can't breathe. I jump out of bed and gasp and sputter, and finally I realize that I am breathing, but my throat is so dry that it hurts. I go to the bathroom, where I guzzle lukewarm water straight from the faucet. And I wonder if this feeling isn't a side effect of drinking too much tonight, like maybe I'm about to have a heart attack or something.

By the time I go back to my room, I am wide awake and know that I won't be falling asleep anytime soon. I am also feeling seriously freaked about what might be the effects of too much alcohol. I decide to go online again and read up on the possibilities. Maybe I can scare myself into straightening up. So I surf and read. I read about things like liver damage, heart failure, and alcohol poisoning, and I am somewhat shocked to learn that you can simply pass out and die from drinking too much. Or worse yet, you could black out and then barf and choke to death on the vomit. Okay, that totally grosses me out. I turn off my computer and go back to bed.

And that's when I promise myself that I will never, ever do this stupid thing again. I will never drink enough to become intoxicated. Maybe I should promise myself never to drink again at all, but that might be going too far.

I consider making a promise to God, but something stops me. Maybe it's that feeling that I am turning into a real hypocrite. Or maybe it's because I think I'm still on my "spiritual vacation." Finally I am able to put all this information and everything else out of my mind and go to sleep.

But I feel like crud in the morning. My head hurts and my mouth tastes like dog vomit. I brush my teeth and use my strongest mouthwash, but it's like this creepy taste just won't go away.

"No breakfast?" asks my mom as I head through the kitchen.

"Not today."

"Feeling okay?"

I shrug. "I didn't sleep too well."

She frowns. "That's too bad. I hope you girls didn't study too late."

"No, that's not it."

"Do you think your new job is wearing you out?"

I brighten. "No, I probably just need to get moving. I'm sure I'll feel better."

"Well, have a good day and don't wear yourself out."

"Thanks."

As I head to my car, I wonder if she notices that I've been avoiding eye contact lately. I mean, I'm sure I've been doing this for nearly a week now, but it's like parents must not pay much attention to those kinds of details—at least I hope they don't.

I am relieved to see that Claire looks no worse for wear this morning. I had been seriously worried that she might've gotten into a wreck last night.

"So you made it home safe," I say as she climbs into my car.

"Of course." She grins. "I always do."

"But doesn't it worry you sometimes?" I ask.

"Yeah, kind of. I guess I feel better when someone else—someone a little more sober—is doing the driving. I mean, I'm not stupid. I know something could go wrong. And if I get pulled over again, well, I just don't want to think about that."

I consider telling her about the information I found on the Web last night, but to be honest, I can barely remember what it was I read—except that it was freaky. I suppose I was still somewhat wasted at the time. *Note to self: Do not attempt alcohol research while drunk.*

Claire changes the subject as I drive us to school, and I must admit, I like her choice of topics much better.

"What are you going to wear on Saturday?" she asks. "Do you have any ideas?"

"I hadn't really thought about—"

"You better think about it. This is your chance to pull out your best threads and really look hot. Know what I mean?"

"Not exactly."

"Well, I may have to come to the aid of the fashion impaired." She pauses to study me. "You're a little taller and skinnier than me, but I might have something that will work for you. Can you stop by after work?"

"That'll be too late," I say quickly. "My parents expect me home by nine thirty." I'm actually relieved since I don't exactly like the idea of being at her house and the likelihood of being offered a drink again. I have no doubt that Claire actually drinks on a daily basis. For all I know, she drinks on an hourly basis.

"Okay, maybe we can figure out how to get you some things tomorrow. Maybe after work or something."

"That'd be great." I'm not sure why I don't tell her I have Friday off. Maybe it's because I'm afraid she'll plan something—something that won't be so good. It amazes me how I am really drawn to this friendship with Claire and how at the same time she sometimes gives me the heebie-jeebies. Kinda freaky.

I park my car, and the two of us head toward school. It's weird, but I have this sudden urge to ask Claire about how much she really drinks, because I do remember reading this one thing last night about teen alcoholism. At the time it seemed pretty far-fetched to me, like *how can a teenager be an alcoholic*? but now I'm feeling kind of curious. I'm about to say something, but she beats me to it.

"Hey, did you finish your English lit project yet?" she asks suddenly.

"Yeah."

"Do you think I could look at it? Not to copy, but just for some inspiration. Mine just seems to be falling flat."

Well, everything in me is saying, "Don't do this," but like an idiot, I hand over the paper that I just finished the other day. "How will you be able to get yours done in time for class?" I ask.

She just shrugs. "I don't know. But I gotta pull this off if I want to pass. Thanks so much, Amber. I promise to give it back to you right before class."

I don't see Claire again before lit class, but that's not so strange since we don't have any other classes together. I wait outside the classroom for her, but finally the bell rings and it's time to go in. Thinking that I might've missed her and that she's already in class, I look for her inside. But she's not there. Neither is my paper.

I don't know what to do. I keep watching the door, thinking she'll come in late. But the hall looks deserted. I lean over and ask Haley if she's seen Claire.

Haley nods with wide eyes and whispers. "Yeah, she's up to it again."

"Up to it?"

"She must've put away about a fifth of vodka this morning. She was a mess in history class. She told Mrs. Lenox she was sick, and I took her to the bathroom."

"Something you'd like to share with the class, ladies?" Mr. Sorenson is looking directly at us.

We both shake our heads and sit back in our seats. Now he is asking for our assignments, and I don't know what to do. I could pretend to be sick. I actually do feel sick. Or I could make something up—yeah, like my dog ate it. That should go over nicely.

"Miss Conrad?" He's standing over me now with his hand out.

"I—uh—I must've lost it. I thought for sure it was in my bag, but it's not there."

His expression is one of boredom and disbelief. "That's too bad, considering this assignment is worth one-fourth of your grade, Miss Conrad."

I swallow hard and look down at my desk without answering.

Then he clears his throat, "But should you miraculously find it, I will mark it down only two marks for being late."

Two marks? That would make an A into a C. Not that I can be sure I even have an A. But I was hoping for at least a high B. And to qualify for the church scholarship, I have to pull at least a B out of this class. Now I'm feeling seriously freaked.

Suddenly Claire is coming into the room. Okay, she looks like crud and her face is white as a ghost, but she is waving some papers in her hand.

"Mr. Sorenson," she says in that sweet voice that she knows how to use so well. "I just found this paper mixed up in my things. Amber gave me a ride this morning, and I must've picked it up by mistake."

He frowns at her. "And why are you late?"

She makes a pained face. "I was in the health room. I'm sick today, and Mrs. Wiley was about to send me home when I found Amber's paper." She hands him the paper. "I thought I should get it to you."

He nods as if this is completely understandable.

"Well, if you are that sick, you should get out of here before we all get exposed to your germs." And to my amazement, he doesn't even ask her about *her* paper!

But I'm mostly relieved that she came through for me. Haley tosses me a surprised glance, like she never expected to see Claire do something like that for a friend. I guess I'm pleasantly surprised too, and now I realize that I need to forgive Claire for this little scare. I mean, I was ready to really tear into her. But now I realize that it's not really her fault—well, not exactly. Even so, that was close!

twelve

I FEEL LIKE I'M WALKING A TIGHTROPE SOMETIMES, LIKE ONE MISSTEP and I'm toast. The problem is that I really want to continue being Claire's friend. I mean, she's fun and funny and exciting and kind of edgy. But at the same time, I don't want to alienate Simi. Even though she's kind of preachy and stuffy, I really do love her, and she's been my best friend for years. But beyond that, I don't want Simi or Lisa or any other youth-group kid to leak out that I've been hanging with the "wrong" kids, because I know that's what they're thinking. I also know they're probably all praying for me like crazy. I'm sure they think I'm some messed-up excuse of a Christian, like some demented sheep that has strayed from the flock and is about to become the big bad wolf's dinner. I know that's what they think. And in some ways, I'd just like to show them.

The good news is that I haven't had a drink since the night Claire came to my house and we both got wasted. Even today when she insisted on taking me to Merenda's for lunch and then offered to order two glasses of wine so that I could drink one with her, I refused. I was seriously tempted to have some wine—not because I wanted to drink it, although I might not have minded loosening up a bit, but because I thought it would feel kind of risky and grown-up to be sitting there drinking a glass of wine when someone like Haley or Stacy or Megan just happened in, which they didn't.

But when Mrs. Bannister (the drama teacher) walked into the deli, I just about died right there on the spot. Claire's back was to the door, so I tried to convey by eye contact that she better watch out. Claire, as cool as could be, picks up her wine glass (carefully so it's in front of her and can't be seen from behind) and downs it all in one long swig and then discreetly slips her glass into the foliage of the potted plant that was right next to her. Pretty smooth. But trust me, my adrenaline was rushing.

So now it's time for the track meet, and by now I've broken down and told Claire that I don't work today, so we're planning to hang together. But I'm still getting this tightrope-walking feeling, like I'd better watch my step. I'm waiting for her at the entrance of the stadium so we can sit together, but I'm thinking she should've been here by now. Then I see her coming toward me. She's got two soft-drink cups in her hands, but she's not coming from the concession stand.

"I got you a Dr Pepper," she says as she hands me my cup, "and I've got red licorice in my purse."

"Cool," I say as we begin to traipse up the stairs. But I have this feeling that I may not be carrying a straight Dr Pepper. Even so, I can't exactly ask, since there are kids and parents and teachers all over the place.

Claire leads us over to where Haley and Stacy and some of her other friends are sitting, and we sit down on the bleacher behind them. The girls turn around and greet us and then focus their attention back out onto the field, where it looks like they're getting ready to run a hurdles event.

I glance nervously at Claire, but she seems to be avoiding my eyes. Then I take a tentative drink. I'm surprised that it tastes pretty much okay, although it isn't exactly what a Dr Pepper should taste like and I do suspect she's spiked it with something—maybe vodka, since it has the least bitter taste. I give her an elbow as if to question this, and she just turns and winks at me. And then I know.

Even so, I take another drink. I realize that absolutely no one has the faintest idea that the two of us are sitting here drinking booze, and I have to admit that kind of amuses me. Okay, maybe I am seriously twisted.

We eat some licorice and continue sipping our drinks, and in my opinion the track meet becomes way more interesting. We stand and loudly cheer for Slater, and the other girls join in, and it's like Slater has his own personal cheering section. He looks up to the stands after winning a race and waves, and we cheer even louder.

To my relief, our drink cups are finally empty, but worried that someone might still discover the secret of our jollity, I gather them both and dispose of them in a nearby trash can. Then, following Claire's lead, I pop in a breath mint. All in all, it's the best track meet I've ever gone to, but I'm not sure if it's the alcohol or me. Slater wins two out of three of his races. I think he takes second in the other one, and all the other guys seem to be doing really well too. When the whole thing is over, it turns out that we have won. South Ashton High has defeated its crosstown rival, North Ashton High. Everyone from our school is ecstatic. Claire and I rush down to the field to congratulate the team, and, of course, we both give Slater a hug.

He seems genuinely happy that I came, and he even thanks me. Then we hug again, and to my surprise we actually kiss. We KISS!!! Right down there in full public view. And I'm not sure if I'm the one who initiates this kiss, or if he does, but I do feel slightly shocked—okay, happy shocked. Then Slater leans over and whispers in my ear.

"I see you girls are starting the party early."

"Party?"

He grins. "Yeah, aren't you coming to the celebration party tonight?" He turns to Claire. "Have you heard about it yet? Some of the guys started planning it when it looked like we might win. It's going to be a kegger down at the reservoir. You girls coming?"

Claire looks at me. "Are we coming?"

I shrug. "Yeah, I guess so." Okay, even as I say this, I know it's a bad idea—a very bad idea. But it's like I can't help myself. It's like I'm on this ride that's just going all on its own.

But Claire has already pulled a twenty out of her purse and discreetly given it to Slater. "Here's our contribution," she says with a grin.

"We should get something to eat," I tell Claire as we leave the meet. "I really need some solid food in my stomach."

She nods. "Yeah, that's a good idea."

And so we go to Pizza Hut and split a small cheese pizza, and by the time we finish, I feel better—and worse. I feel better knowing that the food has helped to sober me up, but I feel worse to think that I agreed to go to a kegger down at the reservoir. I've heard about these parties, and I've heard it can get out of hand. And I'm feeling a little freaked to think of what my parents would say if they knew. Finally I decide to express these feelings to Claire.

"Don't worry," she says. "I know a special place to park. Even if the party did get raided, we could get away."

"But I don't like the whole idea," I admit. "I mean, something about all those kids down there, drinking and being near the water and then driving. Well, it's a little freaky, you know?"

She laughs now. "Man, you think way too hard about this stuff. Why don't you leave that kind of worrying for the old folks? You're a kid, Amber. Start acting like it."

I'm a kid? I'm an adult? Which is it, really? I'm just about to state another objection when Claire cuts me off.

"Look, Amber, you don't have to drink anything, if that's what's worrying you. Maybe you can just be the DD."

"The DD?"

"The designated driver. That way you know we'll get home safely and on time. I really want to go to this party. And besides that, I think Slater really wants you to go too. I saw that kiss."

I kind of smile. "Yeah. I guess I could go and be the DD. But you have to promise to get a ride with someone else if you want to stay late."

"No problem."

So I call home and tell my mom that we won the track meet and that I'm going with Claire to a victory party. Not even a lie this time. And she seems genuinely happy for me as she says, "Have a good time." Well, okay.

When we get to the reservoir, it's obvious that a lot of cars are there. I'm guessing at least thirty. And just as she promised, Claire shows me a secluded place to park that is hard to see from the road. It means we have to walk a little farther, but it seems worth it.

Now, here's what's kind of funny—at least *I* think it's funny. No one else seems to see the humor. When we get to the "party," there are about fifty kids there, and everyone is like waiting for something to happen. There is no keg. Apparently, as the story goes, the money had been collected and then handed over to the "responsible" adult who was going to do the purchasing of the keg, but then the keg never showed.

We hang around for a while, listening to everyone grumbling and complaining, and it's not long before the guys are blaming each other, and the celebration party starts feeling pretty gloomy.

"Kent called his older brother," says Slater, "and he might bring out a couple cases of beer."

Claire just laughs. "A couple of cases isn't going to do much for this crowd." Then she turns to me. "Let's get out of here."

Slater looks clearly disappointed, but Claire reminds him that we have plans for tomorrow.

He nods. "Yeah, come to think of it, I'm kind of tired. Maybe I'll head out too."

And that's when most of the kids start to split. Some of the die-hards remain behind, continuing to claim that "the beer's gonna show up any minute." But I'm just as glad to get out of there.

"What do you want to do?" asks Claire.

"I don't know."

Claire slaps her forehead. "We almost forgot."

"Forgot what?"

"We were going to get you an outfit for tomorrow night. Let's go to my house and you can pick something out." She glances at her watch. "Or if that doesn't work, maybe we'll have time to go to the mall."

Due to the current shape of my finances, I'm not too eager to go to the mall. "Oh, I'm sure we'll find something in your closet," I say quickly. "If you're sure you don't mind."

"Of course I don't mind. This'll be fun."

Now, even as I drive to her house, I am giving myself this little silent lecture: *You will not have a drink—not one single drink—no matter what she does to encourage you. You will not give in.* And strangely enough, I think it's working.

The house is quiet, and Claire finds a note on the breakfast bar. "Big surprise," she says. "They've gone out."

And no surprises here, she heads straight for her green vase, extracts the key, and opens the bar. "What'll you have?" she asks.

"How about a Sprite," I say.

"Yeah, but what do you want in it?"

"Just give it to me straight." I kind of smile.

She just shrugs. "Okay, whatever."

Now this surprises me. I expected more of a protest. But she pulls out a Sprite, pours it over some ice, and hands it to me.

I sip my Sprite and watch as she mixes herself some strange concoction that has just about everything but the barroom sink in it. I'm pretty sure she must be making up the recipe as she goes along.

"What on earth is that?" I finally ask as she pours this mysterious dark-brown mixture into a tall glass of ice and then adds a lemon.

"Long Island iced tea," she says and then takes a swig. "Yummy."

I frown. "Yeah, I'll bet."

"It is."

"Yeah, sure, I'll take your word for it."

"You don't believe me?"

I laugh. "I believe you'd drink anything, Claire. Even if it tasted like paint thinner."

She holds out the tall glass now. "Here, take a sip and see for yourself."

"But I said—"

"Hey, all I said was one sip. I'm not trying to get you plastered. I know you're getting worried about driving and stuff. And to be honest, I am too. But one little sip is not going to hurt."

So I take a sip, and to my surprise, it does taste good. "Okay, you were right," I admit.

Then she gets that sly grin. "You want one?"

"No . . ."

"Oh, you do, don't you?"

I shake my head. "No, not really."

"How about just a little one?"

"A little one?"

"Here, I'll pour a little of mine into a small glass."

Before I can stop her, she's done this and is handing it to me. "Okay," I say to her. "I'll drink this only if you promise not to offer me another—*and* if you lock up the bar right now."

"Okay. I'll lock it up right after I remake the other half of my drink."

So I wait and take turns sipping on my Sprite and my "tea" as she goes back to work mixing another one. Then, respecting my wishes, she puts everything away and locks the bar. "How about if I put the key away for safekeeping?" I suggest.

"What? You don't trust me?"

"Do you trust *me*?"

She shrugs and hands me the key, which I pocket. Later when she's not looking, I put it beneath the green vase instead of inside it. I figure I can tell her later.

Then we go to her room and I am amazed to see the size of her closet. Not only is it a walk-in, it's about the same size as my bedroom. I'm sure my eyes are huge, and she seems amused. I have a feeling I'm not her first friend to react like this. "Whoa," I say as I sit down on a bench that's inside her closet. "This is incredible."

"Well, don't be too impressed. Most of the clothes in here suck. I really need to clean it out."

Soon we are experimenting with various outfits and I'm feeling a little like Cinderella. And the good news is that the more

Claire focuses on fashion, the less she focuses on her beverage. In fact, I notice that her drink is still half full—a good sign, I'm thinking.

So finally we've put together this really hot outfit, and Claire sits down and finishes her drink. Mine is long gone by now, and I'm feeling a little too happy, and I know that it's partly due to the alcohol. And as much as I hate the idea of driving impaired—I mean, didn't I make a promise to myself?—I also don't like the idea of sticking around and being talked into getting totally plastered, so I tell Claire that I have to get home.

"If I'm late tonight, I won't be able to go out tomorrow night," I remind her as I head out.

"Okay," she says. "But before you go, you better tell me what you did with that key."

"Huh?"

"Don't mess with me, Amber." Her blue eyes get dark and serious. *"Where's the key?"*

I blink as I try to remember what key exactly and then where it was that I hid it. Luckily, it all comes back to me, and her face softens with relief when I tell her. Even so, it was kind of freaky. I've never seen Claire get mad like that before.

"Drive safely," she calls as I head out the front door. The irony of this mostly goes over my head, but not completely. And I do think it's a little twisted the way we're always telling each other to "drive safely" when we both know that we're driving under the influence. Like, how safe is that?

But as I get behind the wheel, I tell myself that I've consumed only half a drink. How could that possibly impair my driving ability? In fact, I think I am driving better than ever as I direct my car toward home. But even so, I feel guilty.

While I wait at the traffic light, I pop a breath mint in my mouth just in case my parents are paying attention tonight, which as it turns out, they are not. Man, parents can be so dense sometimes.

thirteen

SIMI IS IN GOOD SPIRITS AT WORK TODAY. SHE'S NOT ON MY CASE ABOUT Claire or anything, and I think that's odd since Simi and I usually hang together on Friday nights and I know I kind of blew her off (again) last night—well, not officially. But I didn't call her or anything, and this would usually make her a little grumpy. To be honest, it would make me grumpy too—well, back before I started hanging with Claire.

Finally I can't stand it any longer and I have to ask. "So, did you have a good time working by yourself last night?"

She smiles mysteriously as she wipes down the inside of the caramel-corn machine. "Wouldn't *you* like to know?"

Okay, that's the kind of thing that annoys me. I mean, why can't she just come out and answer like a normal person? But I play along. "Let me guess," I say. "Brad Pitt left Jennifer Aniston so he could meet you at the mall for coffee?"

She smiles. "Close."

"Come on," I urge. "What's up with you?"

"I had a visitor last night."

"Who?"

"Someone from another school."

"Seriously?" I peer at her, wondering when she's had time to meet a guy from another school.

"He's my neighbor."

"You mean that cute guy with the old BMW?"

"That's the one."

"Tell me everything!"

Fortunately, the shop's not busy just now, so Simi tells her story while I clean little fingerprints off the candy case.

"His name is Andrew Ferris and he's a senior at North."

"Oh, no," I say in mock disgust. "You're interested in a guy from North!"

"Get over it. Besides, I live over there now. It's only natural that I should meet some of the natives." She straightens the trays of candy inside the case and continues talking. "We got to talking a couple days ago, and it turns out he's a Christian. He goes to a Baptist church downtown, and he's really nice. He just happened to pop in last night and we talked. That's all. But I think he's going to ask me out." She closes the candy case and stands up straight. "If I ever get a night off, that is."

"I'll cover for you," I offer.

She nods. "Okay, I might have to hold you to that promise."

Something about that makes me feel bad, like maybe she can't hold me to other promises. Maybe I can't even hold myself to a promise anymore.

"Why don't you go out with him tonight?" I say suddenly. "I mean, since Jan's coming back to let us off early."

"What about youth group?"

"Oh, yeah." I nod like I totally forgot it was Saturday.

"Besides, what am I supposed to do, ask him out?"

"No, I guess that's not a good idea. You don't want to look desperate or anything."

"Right."

"Well, that's cool, Simi. I hope Andrew turns out to be a great guy."

She frowns now. "Like Slater?"

"Slater's a cool guy," I tell her. "You just need to get to know him."

"Seems a little stuck-up if you ask me."

I shake my bottle of Windex at her. "That's because you don't know him. Did you know that he's actually pretty shy? And shy people can sometimes come across as snobs."

"You mean like you?"

"People think I'm a snob?"

"Duh."

I consider this. "Well, some of us socially challenged people need a little help. We need to build up our confidence, you know."

"Do you mean with alcohol?" She looks slightly worried.

"No, that's *not* what I mean," I say quickly since I really don't want to go down that road today. "I guess I just need to practice being more friendly." I study her now. "Like I'm always trying to figure out how you do it, Simi. You're such a natural when it comes to talking to people."

"Must be the Italian blood." She laughs. "Everyone on my dad's side of the family is kind of loud, you know—extroverts."

"Well, I wish I had some of that blood," I say. But now we have customers: a clump of what appear to be middle-school girls with too much makeup and an attitude. I decide to let Simi take them on. I mean, if anyone can tame middle-school girls, it's her.

Finally it's six thirty, and Jan shows up to relieve us. "Have fun at youth group," she says and then laughs. "If that's even possible."

Simi frowns. "It is fun, Aunt Jan. You should give church a try someday. It beats hanging at the bars."

Jan bops her niece on the head with an empty caramel-corn box. "I don't hang out at bars!"

"You know what I mean."

Then Simi and I go out the back door and walk toward our cars. I'm feeling like I want to hurry and better not show it. Simi pauses in front of her little orange Bug and then calls out. "Hey, Amber, is it okay if I change clothes at your house since it's on the way to the church?"

Crud! I try to think of some good excuse but finally realize I better come clean—well, sort of clean. No way am I telling Simi about Lola's.

"Actually, I'm not going home," I admit.

"You're going to youth group wearing that?" she says with amusement since she knows I hate this white-shirt-and-black-pants outfit, not to mention the smell.

"Nooo . . ." I open my car and turn and look at her. "Actually, I have a date tonight."

"Wow, thanks for telling me." Her expression is hurt now.

"I was going to, but then those wild girls came in, and I guess I just forgot."

"Is it with Slater?"

I nod and jangle my keys, a hint that I need to go.

"But you're not going home?"

Gulp. I better think of something. "Well, actually, I have some clothes in my car. I was going to meet him and then change. We're kind of in a hurry, you know. I thought it would save time."

She nods but looks unconvinced. "Yeah, whatever."

"Don't be mad at me," I say in a wimpy voice.

"I'm not mad, Amber." She looks evenly at me. "Maybe just concerned."

"Don't worry," I say. "Everything's fine."

"Well, don't do anything stupid, okay?"

I nod. "I gotta go."

"See ya in church tomorrow?"

"Sure."

Then she gets into her car and I get into mine and I follow her as far as the stoplight, our usual parting place—only this time she turns right toward my house and the church, and I turn left toward her house. I don't know why I turn left, since Claire's house is the other direction, but I guess I just don't want Simi to know where I'm really going. As a result, it takes me a few extra minutes to backtrack to Claire's.

As usual, Claire's mom and stepdad are out, so Claire and I have the house to ourselves. But when she offers me a drink, I flatly refuse.

"I need a clear head," I tell her and then I giggle. "Well, at least while I'm getting dressed. We'll see about later."

She smiles and holds out a card. "Yes, you have to try out your new ID tonight."

I grab the card from her and am surprised to see that it looks a lot like my driver's license, only the background color is different. But upon closer inspection, I see that other than the photo and physical description, quite a bit is different—different name and birth date.

"I'm Ashley Hancock?" I ask in surprise.

"Yeah. You always get a fake name in case the card gets confiscated. That way, they can't track you down. And you have to remember to never, ever show it to a policeman if you get pulled over, or you will be in some seriously deep doo-doo."

I nod and wonder if this whole fake-ID thing is really such a good idea. But suddenly Claire is helping me change and trying out different kinds of jewelry and hairstyles and makeup, and I soon forget all about the ID.

"You look hot, Amber," she says when we're finally done. And I have to agree with her: I *do* look hot. Not only that, but I look older too.

"That skirt looks way better on you than it does on me," she says. "You might as well keep it."

I look down at the black flouncy skirt and nod. "It's a little short, but I guess it's okay."

"It makes your legs look long," she says.

I have to laugh. Being friends with someone like Simi has always made me feel that my legs were short, but compared to Claire, I guess I'm on the leggy side.

"And this top is way cool," I tell her as I admire the twisted neckline that fits so well. "I love this color of purple."

She nods with approval. "I forgot it looks so good. I may not want you to keep that."

"I'll try to take care of it and not sweat too much."

She laughs. "Hey, you can sweat as much as you want."

My hair is pulled into a messy bun that's held in place with some of her hair clips, and I have on these amazing hoop earrings that are way bigger than anything I've worn before. All in all, the look is good. And I'm relieved to say that all this effort has kept Claire occupied and away from her stepdad's bar.

"You look great too," I tell her. "I can't wear pastels like that without looking totally babyish. But on you, they're great."

"I'm going for a Paris Hilton look," she says and then pauses. "Is that the doorbell?"

It's hard to tell over the music that's playing, but we go downstairs to find that Slater is waiting.

"Wow!" he says when we come out. "You both look great. Maybe I should walk into the club with one of you on each arm."

Okay, this comment makes me a little jealous, but not for long.

"Well, you might walk in with a girl on each arm," says Claire as she gets into the backseat of Slater's Accord, "but you'll be walking out with only one later. I plan to be walking out with Eric Bradford."

"Do you think he'll be there?" I ask.

"I *know* he'll be there."

"How do you know?" asks Slater as he opens the passenger door for me.

"I called his cell."

"How'd you get that number?" I ask as I slide into the seat. I can't believe that Slater is such a gentleman!

"I ran into a mutual friend at the mall today, and she had it on her."

"What luck!" I say as Slater pulls out of the driveway.

"Yeah, I'm just a lucky kind of girl."

fourteen

CLAIRE IS THE ONE WHO KEEPS THE CONVERSATION GOING AS SLATER drives to Stanfield. The trip takes about twenty minutes on the freeway, but I can see how it would be a very long twenty minutes with just Slater and me in the car. I am so thankful that Claire is along to keep the conversation moving.

Before long I can see the city lights, and I begin to feel this flutter of excitement rush through me—like okay, let the fun begin! But at the same time, I am getting extremely nervous too, and suddenly I wish I'd had a drink at Claire's house.

"So you guys have done this a lot?" I ask.

"Done what?" says Claire.

"Used fake IDs to get into clubs."

"Oh, yeah," she tells me. "I do it all the time, and I know Slater does it occasionally. Right, Slater? I mean, I've seen you at a few places."

"Yeah, I've done it a few times, but not as much as you. You probably have the record for sneaking into clubs and bars and stuff."

Claire laughs. "And I've never been caught either."

"Any close calls?" I ask, still feeling nervous at the thought of getting caught.

"No. I just act like everything's cool, and then it is."

Okay, this doesn't make me feel any better since my ability to "act cool" is severely challenged once I get panicky. "So if you act cool, no one suspects you're not really twenty-one?"

"Well, think about it, Amber. If you come across as all nervous and jumpy, of course they're going to question your age."

"But what if I can't help it?"

Claire leans forward into the front seat and frowns at me. "Are you chickening out?"

"Not exactly. But I guess I'm just starting to freak a little. I mean, I really don't want to get in trouble."

Claire lets loose with a bad word, and then I hear her digging around in her bag in the backseat. The next thing I know, she's thrusting her silver flask in my face. "You better have a drink, Amber."

"But I—"

"No arguing. You need to loosen up, and Jack's just the guy to help you."

I make a face. "Jack Daniel's?"

"That's the one. Now be a big girl and take a nice long swig."

I glance at Slater, but he's just grinning like this is some funny joke. "You know this hard stuff makes me want to barf, Claire."

"Come on," she urges in a gentler voice. "You can do this, okay? Just take a drink to calm your nerves, and then you'll be fine. Trust me."

So I take a deep breath and then a swig. The liquid burns like fire in my mouth and all the way down my throat, and my eyes immediately begin to water. But oddly enough, it doesn't taste quite as nasty as it did the first time she had me do this, even though I'm still coughing and gasping a little.

"I've got some leftover soda in this cup," offers Slater. "It's probably flat but—"

"I'll take it." I grab the cup and drink a big gulp of the tasteless Coke.

"Take another swig," insists Claire after I try to give the flask back to her. "I know that one little drink is not going to cut it with you."

"But—"

"No buts. If you blow this tonight, we could all go down with you. Come on, Amber, you have to get your act together for the sake of the group."

"Yeah," says Slater. "If they see us together and then pull your ID, they'll probably pull ours too. And then we gotta get outta there fast."

"And I don't want to make you feel bad, but a fake ID is not cheap, Amber."

So, feeling like the fate of the evening is riding on my shoulders, I take another swig. At least I have the stale Coke ready to wash it down.

"Good girl," says Claire as she takes back the flask. "You need any, Slater?"

"Not yet," he says as he exits the freeway. "But I'll have some before we go in."

I lean back and attempt to relax, and by the time Slater has parked the car, I'm feeling like a new woman. I laugh as Slater takes a couple of drinks from Claire's flask, teasing him when he sputters a little.

"Hey, I'm not as bad as you," he says and then takes another swig.

"Well, I'm still a novice," I say as we get out and walk toward a brightly lit building with an exterior that's painted in garish shades of acid green and turquoise.

"Hey, that makes my bedroom look pretty tame," I say to Claire.

She laughs. "Yeah, you should see her bedroom, Slater. You'd think she was a real wild woman at heart."

Slater smiles and takes my hand. "I guess that's what I was hoping."

We get in a roped-off line filled with people who look anywhere from thirteen to thirty—not that I'm a good judge of ages. I'm not. And as I compare us to the others, I think we look believable, but as we get nearer to the entrance, I feel a little uneasy.

Claire is totally comfortable. She's laughing and joking like this is no big deal. And Slater is still holding my hand, which I have to admit is quite comforting. Then just as we get to the front, Claire launches into this hilarious description of a recent episode of this fairly raunchy reality-TV show. And it's like everyone around us is listening and laughing, and when we get to the big guy who's carding, he pauses to listen to her monologue and then throws back his head and laughs. And like no big deal, he casually checks our IDs, lets us pass, and says, "Hope you enjoy the show."

And just like that, we are in and I'm thinking, *Hey, this is pretty cool. It's like we really are grown-ups—like we passed some kind of test.* The place is already getting packed, and we go up some stairs to a kind of balcony thing and stand at one of those tall little tables, where some other people are already standing around and sipping drinks.

"What do you guys want?" Slater has to yell to be heard above the music, which I've already been informed is just the warm-up band and not DistanceWalker (the underground British band that Claire is so certain will become the Beatles of the new millennium—yeah, right).

Claire orders a Long Island iced tea and I figure that sounds like a fairly safe bet, so I order the same. Then Slater goes off to wait in line at the bar.

"Have you seen Eric yet?" I ask Claire.

She just shakes her head and continues searching through the crowd. Man, I hope this guy shows up. I know she's going to be bummed if he doesn't. Then I ask her when DistanceWalker is going to play, and she says probably not until nine or later.

"That late?"

She nods, looking at me like I'm slightly retarded. "That's not that late, Amber."

"Yeah, yeah."

It's hot in here, and my sandals are starting to feel tight. They're actually Claire's sandals and a half-size too small, although they seemed okay when I was walking across the thick white carpet in her bedroom. Not only that, but the heels are like four inches high and the balls of my feet are starting to burn.

"Is there any place to sit?" I ask her.

She shrugs and points to where some others are starting to sit on the stairs. *Great,* I'm thinking. But then I remind myself, *Hey, you're supposed to be having fun!*

It feels like about an hour before Slater comes back with our drinks, although it's probably more like fifteen minutes. How he managed to get the tray through the crowd without spilling too much is a mystery to me, but the tall glass of "tea" with lemon looks appealing since the warm room is making me pretty thirsty.

The three of us click our glasses in a toast that Claire makes but I can't hear. Then I take a drink. Of course, I realize this drink has alcohol in it, but somehow I convince myself that it doesn't have that much. It tastes a lot better than what's in Claire's flask, and it's not long before my glass is empty.

Slater looks slightly surprised but politely asks if I want another drink. I feel kind of greedy when I say yes. Then I actually hold up my little purse that has only my ID and a twenty-dollar bill (since Claire said not to bring anything else in case I lose it) and offer to pay for the next round.

"No way," he tells me. "Put that away."

"You can just get me a Coke or Dr Pepper," I tell him.

"Don't you want another Long Island?"

I shrug.

Then he grins. "Sure, you do. We all do. Right, Claire?"

She holds up her almost-empty glass. "Count me in."

So off he goes to wait at the bar again. But this time it's taking longer and the crowd is thicker, and while he's gone, Claire spots Eric and takes off to say hello. So now I am standing by myself and feeling a little tipsy—tipsy but happy. Suddenly the music sounds better, and I'm feeling pretty relaxed.

Before I know it, I'm talking to complete strangers—a girl named Amy who lives in Stanfield and her boyfriend, Peter, who's from out of town.

We're all talking loudly so we can be heard over the music, and it's not long before I'm so relaxed that I nearly let it slip that I'm still in high school. But just before I blow it completely, I recover and tell them that I just graduated from college. And then, pretending that I'm Simi's sister Lena (although I don't use her name), I tell them the things that Lena has done as though it were me. I tell them that my major was counseling and that I just moved back home to save money, and they nod as if this is totally believable. They seem like nice people, and I introduce them to Slater when he comes back.

Then he points to a place to sit that has just been vacated, and I'm so happy that I run and sort of stumble on my way over. I get there just in time. As soon as I sit down, I take off the painful sandals, and although the floor is sticky and gross, my feet are so relieved that I don't even care.

"Good save," says Slater as he joins me. He clears a place on the messy table so that he can set our drinks down. "Where's Claire?"
I point to where I last saw her, but I don't actually see her now. "She found Eric," I say as he hands me my second Long Island. We hold our glasses in another toast "to a fun night," and then I take a long, cool sip.

Okay, it starts getting a little blurry here. In some far corner of my brain, I realize that I haven't had anything to eat since my lunch break at the mall, and that was just a big pretzel and a medium Orange Julius. Not only that, but I've just consumed not only two but two and a half Long Island iced teas (since Slater and I decided to split Claire's), and I'm starting to feel a little strange—or maybe the room's starting to move now.

I have no idea how much time has passed, but I try to keep a brave front for Slater's sake. I'm pretty sure that DistanceWalker has taken the stage, since the lighting has changed and there's something up there making smoke and stuff.

Off and on, I think I'm talking to Slater, making intelligent comments about the band, although I'm not really sure that I'm making sense. I'm not actually sure about much of anything. I'm not even sure if I'm still here or not. Everything is becoming this dark, noisy, smoky blur.

Then suddenly, like out of the blue, I feel like I'm going to hurl. And it's like I can't breathe and I can hardly see, and although I'm on my feet, it feels as if I'm tilting sideways and falling.

When I come to, I am in the bathroom with the girl I'd met earlier—was it Amy?—and she's holding a wet paper towel on my forehead.

"What happened?" I ask, or at least that's what I mean to say. It sounds like "wha-happen?" to my ears.

"You passed out," she tells me. "Your boyfriend asked me to help get you in here. He thought you were going to lose your cookies."

"Did I?" I ask hopefully.

She shakes her head no and then frowns.

Then I close my eyes and wish I were dead.

"Do you want me to call someone?" I hear her asking, but it's kind of fuzzy like maybe I'm imagining it.

"Call God," I say, and I think that makes her laugh. But the trouble is, I am perfectly serious.

"Are you going to be okay?" she asks when I finally open my eyes again, but I think I see two of her. Does she have a twin?

"Yeah," I tell her as I try to stand up. "Don' worry 'bout me." But as I make it to my feet, everything starts to spin again and I feel woozy and barfy and I'm looking for a place to throw up. I see what looks like about a waist-high trash can and I stagger over and make it just in time.

I'm not sure how long I stand there hanging on to the trash can and barfing, but the next thing I know, I feel like I really need to use the toilet. And I'm not talking about just taking a little whiz. I mean, it feels like I'm getting diarrhea—full-blown "I'm-gonna-explode" diarrhea.

But every stall seems to be occupied, and finally I am standing there yelling for someone to vacate or else I'm going to lose it right there on the floor—and it's going to be ugly and smelly and gross.

A girl shoots out of a stall, and I manage to go in. As I close the door, I hear another girl saying how they shouldn't let *some people* into clubs. "They ruin it for everyone," she says loudly as I barely make it down on the toilet seat on my second attempt.

"Some people just don't know how to drink," says another girl.

"Some people shouldn't be allowed on the streets after dark," says another, and they all laugh like it's funny.

But let me tell you, that bathroom gets pretty quiet after the smells from my stall start seeping out. And I'm pretty sure it is nearly evacuated as I sit there and moan and groan, holding my throbbing head with both my hands and wishing I could just get this over with and die. Finally I think I'm done, and I do feel just a tiny bit better, but all I want to do is go home—and die.

I look down at these filthy bare feet on the nasty bathroom floor and it takes me a minute to realize that they belong to me. Then suddenly my stomach is twisting and turning, and I feel like I'm going to barf again.

"God, help me," I mumble as I realize what a pathetic, messed-up loser I am. Is it possible that only a few weeks ago I was living a completely sane and normal life and now I'm just one step away from needing to be hauled out of this place in an ambulance? I make myself sick.

Tears are streaming down my face as I cling to the filthy toilet and wait to vomit again, and the whole time I'm thinking, *Are we having fun yet? What was I thinking to get into such a mess? I am such a fool, such a stupid fool.*

I don't know how much time passes, but I somehow manage to pull myself together enough to make it out of the bathroom. Slater finds me sitting on a step just outside the door and asks if I'm okay.

I tell him that I want to go home, or at least that's what I'm trying to say. It comes out in these messy sobs that probably don't make much sense. But somehow he gets it, and to my surprise, he doesn't seem to mind that I've ruined the evening for everyone.

I don't know where Claire's sandals are and think it's hopeless to even try to find them, but Slater helps me walk out to the car without stepping on anything too disgusting. Feeling totally lame, I apologize about a dozen times as we're walking. Then once I'm safely tucked into the passenger seat, he announces that he's going back inside to tell Claire. I'm disappointed that we're not leaving right away but sober enough to realize we can't just abandon Claire either.

"Will you be okay for a few minutes?" he asks as he locks the doors.

"Don' worry," I say. "I'll jus' take a li'l nap."

I don't wake up until Slater starts helping me out of the car, and I'm afraid he's taking me back into Lola's. But then my feet are on something wet and cold. I look down and see what looks like grass.

"Where am I?" I mutter.

"Your house," he tells me.

Now, *there's* a somewhat sobering thought. I mean, I am definitely relieved to be home, but I can't imagine how I'm going to explain all this to my parents—especially when they think I've been at youth group tonight. Youth group, ha-ha! Pretty funny.

He walks me up to the side door that I've pointed out and then, pausing briefly, kisses me on the forehead. "I'm sorry you got sick," he says.

"I'm sorry too," I say for like the hundredth time.

Then I open the door and tiptoe into the semidark house and stand in the kitchen for a minute or two just holding my breath and waiting to become toast. I'm not sure what makes me think my parents would be up, since on a normal Saturday night they would have already gone to bed by now, and I can see by the kitchen clock that it's after eleven. Of course, this has not been a normal night—at least not for me.

For some irrational reason, I think that if tonight's been such a horrible ordeal for me, well, then everyone else must know what's going on too, like I really do believe it's all about me. But as I slowly move through the house, making my way toward my bedroom while trying not to bump into anything, I assume by the crack of light beneath their door that my parents have already turned in for the night. Oh, I know they're not asleep yet. They just go into their room and read and stuff, and when I get home, at least one of them will say something.

"Good night, Amber," calls my mom.

"'Night, Mom," I call in a voice that doesn't quite sound like mine. I'm guessing my dad has already dozed off. My mom doesn't seem to suspect anything, so I slip into my room and collapse on my bed and, with tears pouring down my hot cheeks, pass out.

Will I ever wake up? Maybe I don't care. And if I wake up, what will I find? What will be left of me? I think I'm in about a thousand pieces right now—pieces that are strung out along I-42 between Ashton and Stanfield. And like Humpty Dumpty, I don't know if I can ever find the pieces and put them back together again. I am a mess.

fifteen

I WAKE UP IN THE MIDDLE OF THE NIGHT AND THINK I'M GOING TO BARF again. I try to be quiet as I go to the bathroom, but I'm shaky and disoriented and I have to hold on to the wall to get there. I sit on the edge of the tub crying. I wish this all would end. I even ask God to help me, and I promise myself and him that I will never touch a drop of alcohol again. I will go to church and youth group and maybe even become a missionary to China or Nigeria.

Then I throw up and have diarrhea all over again. I feel like a dirty dishcloth that's been wrung out again and again. How can there be anything left inside my body? I recall something I read online about alcohol poisoning and how your body reacts to an overdose of alcohol like it's a poison, and I realize that's what I've been doing—I've been poisoning myself! And then I start crying all over again.

I brush my teeth and drink some water and then peer into the mirror above the sink. I look absolutely hideous. It's like I'm a monster. My eyes look like bloodshot slits that have been carved into my blotchy and swollen face. And there are black streaks of eye makeup running down my cheeks. I stare in horrified amazement and tell myself to remember this—to remember this is what it looks like. I think that might help me to never do it again, not that I think I will ever be tempted. I mean, how could a person feel so bad, hit such depths, and then go back for more? No, that's impossible. I know it.

I consider taking a shower, but besides not having the energy, I know it would wake up my mom, and then I'd have to explain. So, feeling filthy and wrung out, I go back to bed and sleep fitfully until morning.

I'm slightly better but not okay as I go back to the bathroom and take a shower. The water feels like needles penetrating my skin so hard that I think I must be bleeding, but I'm not. I'm shaky and breathing hard by the time I get out and towel myself off. But the towel feels like sandpaper and I'm sure that it is tearing up my skin, but it's not.

I put on some clean sweats and crawl back into bed, where I alternate between shivering and getting too hot.

"Amber?" calls my mom. "You coming to church?"

I sit up in bed and do my best to look normal as she peeks in the door. "I've got to be at work an hour early today," I mumble, barely feeling guilty for the lie.

She frowns. "That's too bad. Maybe you should ask for Sundays off after this."

I nod, which makes my throbbing head ache even more. "Yeah, I'll do that."

Then I lie back down and she leaves and I sleep until ten thirty. I get up and slowly get dressed, but I honestly don't know if I can make it into work today. I still feel nauseated and weak and shaky.

I make myself drink a glass of orange juice, which I think tastes a lot like vomit. Then I get in my car and start to drive. But here's what's weird: it's like I'm still under the influence, like I'm still drunk. And it's freaky. It's like it takes all my concentration just to stay on the right side of the street and stop at lights and stuff, and

I'm really scared that I'm going to get in a wreck. Finally I get to the mall and slowly walk to The Caramel Corn Shoppe's back door.

"Hi, Amber," says Jan in a cheerful voice.

"Hi," I answer back as I put my bag underneath the counter.

"You okay?" Now she's peering at me like I must still look pretty awful. "You look like death warmed over," she says.

"Thanks."

"No, really, you look sick. What's wrong?"

"I, uh, I think I have the flu."

"Well, why didn't you call? You can't work in here with the flu, Amber."

"I thought I was getting better."

Now she looks even closer at me, and I can tell by her expression that she's sort of confused. Finally she says, "Have you been drinking, Amber?"

Of course I deny it.

"Well, I didn't really think so, but it was an honest question."

"That's okay."

"Well, you better go home. I can't have you in here looking like that."

"Sorry."

"Maybe I can get Simi to come in earlier. She's supposed to be here at two."

I nod but don't say anything as I pick up my bag to leave.

"I hope you feel better. Call me if you think I need to change next week's schedule."

"Yeah." Then I go back out to my car and get inside and just cry. I honestly can't remember when I've felt as awful as I've felt during these past twelve hours.

I go back to bed when I get home and sleep soundly until nearly two. Amazingly, I feel a lot better when I get up—not quite normal, but way better. I make myself eat a bowl of Rice Krispies with a banana sliced on top, and then I actually start to feel okay. I wonder where my parents are and then realize they probably assumed I was at work and went out for lunch after church.

I go outside and sit on our front porch steps. I'm sitting in the sun, and it feels amazingly good, like a healing touch from the heavens, and it's like I want to thank God for sparing me. Yet I feel so humiliated for having been such an idiot that I can't even pray, so I just sit there and do nothing.

Then a car drives up and I realize it's Slater, and I look so awful that I'm tempted to run in the house and hide. But then I think, *What difference does it make?* I'm sure he thinks I'm a total loser anyway. I mean, I can't believe how I messed everything up last night.

"How you doing?" he asks as he comes up the walk.

"I've been better," I admit.

"Still hung over?"

"I think it's almost gone now."

He sits down beside me and sighs. "I felt pretty cruddy too."

That's when it occurs to me that he'd had as much to drink as me, and yet he drove us home. "Do you feel bad about driving after you've been drinking?"

He nods. "Yeah, but I never think about it at the time. I mean, I always think I'm okay, like I can handle it. And I do. But then, like the next day, I think that it was really stupid, and I tell myself I'll never do it again."

"Yeah, me too."

"But then you do."

I don't say anything.

"I'm sorry you got sick last night," he says. "I felt really bad, like it was kind of my fault, you know?"

"It wasn't your fault, Slater. No one forced me to drink that much."

"But I should've seen it coming. I mean, I know how much alcohol is in a Long Island iced tea."

"How much?"

He kind of laughs now. "You really wanna know?"

I nod.

"Well, okay, there's a shot of tequila, a shot of rum, a shot of gin, a shot of vodka, and a shot of triple sec."

"Are those all alcohol?"

"Yep."

"That's a lot of alcohol."

"Yep."

"How come you know so much about mixing drinks?" I ask.

"My parents like to drink."

"Oh."

"And I guess that's why I feel bad."

"Because your parents drink."

He smiles. "No, because I knew better than to let you drink two and a half Long Island iced teas. I mean, I shouldn't have had that much myself, and I weigh a lot more than you. That's too much."

"Why do we do it?" I ask as much to myself as to him.

"Drink?"

"Yeah."

He shrugs. "Most of the time, I don't drink. I mean, I'm not like Claire or some of the guys I know who have to have a drink first thing in the morning and just keep it going all day long. I couldn't do that."

"Me neither."

"I wouldn't be able to run track if I did."

"I wouldn't be able to do anything."

Now there's a long pause, and it occurs to me that we're actually having a conversation without the assistance of either booze or Claire.

"I guess I drink to fit in," he says, "and to help me loosen up, you know? To talk more."

"You're talking now."

He nods. "That's cool. I mean, I can talk around people I'm comfortable with."

I feel hopeful. "So, does that mean you're comfortable with me?"

He pushes some hair away from my face and really looks at me now. "Yeah."

I don't know what to say.

He sort of laughs now. "I guess you can't help but be comfortable with someone after you've seen them get completely wasted and act like a total fool."

"Thanks."

"But I still like you."

I smile now. "Thanks."

We talk some more, and I'm amazed at how we really seem to understand each other.

"The thing is, I don't want to drink like that," he says. "I mean, I'm not giving it up completely, but I don't want to get drunk. And I don't want to drive under the influence. I think that's incredibly stupid."

"I'm with you, although I have been considering giving it up completely. I even promised myself that I'd never drink again." I don't mention my promise to God. "But then my head was hanging over the toilet at the time."

"Well, I just think we need to be sensible about it. I get worried about people like Claire. She's taken it way too far."

"Do you think she's an alcoholic?"

"You think?"

"Okay. I suppose it's obvious. But it just seems so weird, you know? I guess I assumed that only older people became alcoholics."

"I think anyone can become an alcoholic. I'm pretty sure that my dad is, but he's a functional alcoholic."

"Meaning?"

"He goes to work and stuff, but when he gets home, he starts drinking and doesn't stop until he falls asleep."

"Why do you think he does it?"

Slater just shrugs. "I don't know. It doesn't look like much fun to me."

"Well, I think it's good that you realize this stuff now," I tell him. "It's like you won't make the same mistake."

"I hope not."

I close my eyes and lean my head back, allowing the warmth of the sun to wash over my face. I'm amazed at how good it feels to be alive right now.

"I wanted to ask you something, Amber."

I sit up straight and look at him. "Yeah?"

"I know we don't know each other that well, and last night was pretty much a disaster, but I was kind of wondering if you'd like to go to the prom with me?"

"Seriously?" I feel the excitement behind my voice.

He nods. "I know it's kind of short notice, since the prom's just a couple weeks away and—"

"No problem," I tell him. "I'd love to go."

Now he smiles, and it occurs to me that he has the best smile. Then I throw my arms around him and we hug briefly. Then it's like we're both kind of embarrassed and that old familiar feeling of nervousness and self-consciousness kicks in. And in the worst case of bad timing, my parents pull up, and the next thing I know, they are both standing on the porch and looking curiously at Slater.

I manage to pull off introductions without too much pain, and Slater makes some polite small talk and then says that he has to go. He promises to call me later.

And naturally, this is when my parents start questioning me. I somehow get them off the "why aren't you at work?" inquisition by casually mentioning my latest news—the prom invitation. And then they want to know if Slater is "my boyfriend." *Parents!*

sixteen

I TRY TO AVOID SPENDING MUCH TIME WITH CLAIRE DURING THE NEXT few days. Of course, I do this discreetly, using my job and homework and even Slater as the reasons I can't hang with her more. But as the week draws to an end, I can tell that she's seeing through me.

"What's up with you?" she finally asks me on Thursday. We're in English lit, but it's almost time for class to start.

"What do you mean?"

"It's like you've been snubbing me lately."

"I've just been busy."

"Yeah, whatever." But I can tell that she's hurt, and I don't know what to say.

"And I've been wanting to tell you the latest news," she says.

Okay, this makes me curious. But then the bell rings, and I have to wait until class is over before I can get the scoop.

"What's up?" I ask as soon as we're out in the hall.

"Well, Eric is taking me to the prom."

I smile. "That's great."

"I ended up inviting him, but he was cool with that. He said that he didn't want to go to his own prom anyway since they're doing this Hawaiian theme. Everyone has to dress like a tourist or something. Kind of lame, don't you think? Anyway, we're going to hire a stretch limo. Actually, I've already reserved it. Do you and Slater want to join us? My treat."

"I don't know. I can ask Slater." To be honest, I'm a little uneasy with the idea of going to the prom with Claire and Eric, but at the same time, it would be so awesome to show up in a limo.

"I'll see Slater in my next class," she says quickly. "I can ask him."

There doesn't seem to be any point in protesting. Besides, maybe it's better if Slater makes this decision.

My cell phone rings just as I'm parking my car at the mall. I'm pulling in next to Simi's little orange Bug, and I realize that I'm a couple minutes late for work.

"Amber," says Claire happily. "It's set. Slater is cool with sharing a limo."

"That's great," I tell her. Even so, I'm still wondering if it's really a good idea.

"I think Slater liked the idea of having a designated driver." She laughs.

"Yeah," I say as I hurry across the lot. "That's probably a good thing." Although I am pretty sure that I won't be doing any drinking that night.

"Have you got a dress yet?"

"No. I haven't really had time. But I do get paid today, so I guess I better start looking."

"Why don't we look together?" she says.

Well, I can't think of any good excuse to say no, and besides, I know that Claire would be a great asset when it comes to picking out something that will look good on me. So, eager to get off the phone, I agree, and we decide that we'll go shopping tomorrow afternoon since I'll only be working until one.

"You're late," says Simi when I come in through the back door.

"Sorry," I tell her as I head for the tiny bathroom that I've been using to change into work clothes. "Is Jan here?"

"Lucky for you, she's not."

So I hurry and change and then come back out. "I'll skip my break," I tell Simi as I put on my apron.

"Nah, that's okay," she says, peering at me more closely. "As long as you haven't been out drinking or something."

I roll my eyes. "Go ahead," I tell her, "smell my breath and see."

She laughs. "Thanks, but no thanks."

"So how are things with Andrew?" I ask as I start to wipe down the soda machine.

"Not bad." But I can tell by the twinkle in her eye that this is probably an understatement.

"Did you go to church with him last night?" I ask as I scrub a sticky spot on the counter.

"I did."

"How'd that go?"

"Good." Then she turns and looks at me intently. "He is such a cool guy, Amber. It just seems like a God thing that we got together. It's like we have so much in common and it's so easy to talk with him, like we've known each other forever."

"That's cool." And I guess I feel a little envious because although Slater and I really connected on Sunday, it still feels awkward, and I'm not really sure where I stand. I mean, I know we're going to the prom together, and that's a big thing. But sometimes when we talk, it just seems so hard.

"And last night, he even asked me about the prom."

"He's taking you to the prom?"

"No. We just talked about it. He said his prom isn't very appealing this year."

I laugh. "Yeah, I heard that North is doing a Hawaiian theme."

"So what does that mean? Like coconuts and grass skirts?"

"Yeah. They probably do the hula and wear leis instead of corsages. Anyway, maybe you should invite Andrew to come to our prom."

She makes a face. "Isn't that kind of pathetic?"

"That's what Claire did."

"Yeah, well, she was probably under the influence too."

"That's not fair."

"Sorry."

"Hey, if you and Andrew go to the prom, maybe you could ride with us in the stretch limo."

"You're going in a stretch limo?" Simi actually looks impressed.

"Well, Claire hired it."

"Oh." Now she doesn't look as impressed.

"Hey, it could be fun. And think about it, you and Andrew could be missionaries to the rest of us heathens."

Simi narrows her eyes now. "So you're including yourself on the heathens list now?"

"I just figured everyone else was anyway."

She sighs loudly. "Oh, Amber."

Then we have customers, and I am thankful to have this conversation interrupted. I feel like I've been walking on eggshells with Simi this week. I know that she thinks I'm a big mess, but at least she hasn't been preaching at me. In fact, she's been incredibly gracious. Strangely enough, that makes me feel more guilty than ever, and I wonder if she knows this and is doing it on purpose.

I'm tempted to confess everything to Simi, like my fake ID and how we went to Lola's and how horrible it was when I got sick. But at the same time, I don't know if I want her to know just how low I've gone. I keep telling myself that I'm done with that kind of stupidity, but the problem is, I'm just not sure. And so far, I don't really feel like I've come clean with God yet. In some ways, I feel more lost than ever.

We're both tired when it's time to quit. We don't talk much as we lock up the shop and head out to the parking lot.

"See you tomorrow," I say as we get into our cars.

"Yeah, see ya."

Then we both drive out of there and meet again at the stoplight, where Simi turns left and I turn right. As usual, we wave and go our separate ways, but for some reason, it makes me really sad tonight, like it's some kind of metaphor of where we are in our friendship. But honestly, I don't really want to go our separate ways. I love Simi and want to keep being friends, but I'm just not sure how to do this. It's like I know I need to start making some better choices and need to get my heart right with God—yet I don't.

Simi only works until six the next day, and since we're surprisingly busy, we don't talk much until right before she leaves.

"I'm going out with Andrew tonight," she announces as she hangs up her apron.

"Cool," I say as I shovel some caramel corn into a small box. "You going to ask him about going to the prom?"

She winks at me. "I'm going to pray about it."

"Well, remember Ruth in the Bible. She had to make the first move on Boaz."

Simi laughs. "It's good to hear you still know your Bible." And I can tell by her playful tone she's not being judgmental.

I turn back to the counter, where a middle-aged woman is waiting for her caramel corn and listening with a confused expression.

"Don't mind us," I tell her. "My dad's a preacher and my friend's a religious fanatic."

Simi snaps me with her apron. "For that, I am leaving."

"Have fun," I tell her as I ring up the caramel corn.

Later on I'm happily surprised when Slater shows up. Things have quieted down, and he just hangs around the shop to visit. I figure Jan shouldn't mind since I keep myself busy cleaning the windows while he's there. Besides that, it's easier to be around Slater when I've got something to do besides just stand there and talk. He only stays about twenty minutes, but I think I'm relieved when he finally goes.

The next day, Saturday, Simi and I work together for only an hour before my shift ends. But during that time, I learn that she has asked Andrew to the prom after all and that he told her he'd be honored to take her.

"So did God give you the green light?" I ask her in a slightly teasing voice.

"I had a real sense of peace about it."

"Well, good."

"How about you?"

"Huh?"

"Do you have a sense of peace about going to the prom with Slater?"

I consider this. "I don't know. I guess I never really thought about it like that." The truth is, I don't have a sense of peace about anything. Not only that, but it's really starting to get to me, and although I feel kind of trapped, I also think it's about time to do something about it. I'm just not sure what.

"I also told Andrew what you said about being missionaries and sharing your stretch limo."

"Seriously?"

"Uh-huh. And you know what he said?"

I shake my head.

"He said he wanted to."

"Seriously?"

"Yep. But are you sure that Claire will really want us? I mean, she might think we're a couple of wet blankets."

"Let me ask her," I say. But I don't tell Simi that I've already got plans to go dress shopping with Claire. I know that would hurt Simi's feelings. But had I known Simi was going to the prom, I'd probably have gone shopping with her instead. But what can I do about that now?

"When are you getting your dress?" I ask.

"I think I'll just borrow something from Lena."

"Oh, yeah. She probably has some cool things to choose from."

"And it'll save me some bucks," says my ever-practical friend. "Besides, it seems crazy to buy a dress that's only for one night."

"Lucky that you and Lena are the same size."

"Too bad you're not or she could probably loan you something too."

I laugh. "I'd have to wear eight-inch heels and a corset so tight that I'd probably pass out."

And so when my shift is over, I don't feel quite so guilty about going dress shopping with Claire.

"Have fun," I say as I leave.

"Yeah, right."

Then I drive over to Claire's house, and we head for the good mall. "Let's start with Nordstrom's," she says. "I heard they have a good selection still."

And so we shop and shop, and after going to several stores and then going back to where we started, Nordstrom's, we both find something that works.

The theme of our prom is Hollywood, which we think is much cooler than Hawaii, and our plan is to go with the red-carpet look, which is mainly sophisticated and with lots of bling bling. Of course, my bling is some fake stuff that I got at an accessories store. But Claire plans to borrow some real bling bling from her mother. I just hope she doesn't get so drunk that night that she loses something valuable. But then again, I guess that's not really my problem, right? I have no doubt that she'll be drinking, because the truth is, I have never been around Claire when she's not drinking—or just been drinking. And I also have no doubt that she is an alcoholic.

Claire's dress is a backless pink number that we think looks like something Marilyn Monroe might've worn, and Claire has the right kind of figure for it. My dress is a sleek, classic number in black satin that Claire picked out. She swears it makes me look taller and thinner. I wish. Lucky for me, the saleslady marked the dress down because of a small rip in the side seam, and I'm sure my mom can fix it with no problem. And I plan on getting some cheap shoes at one of those discount shoe stores. Claire showed me several designer styles that cost a fortune at Nordstrom's, but I'm sure I can find an adequate imitation for a whole lot less. All in all, I'm set and feeling happy.

"Thanks for helping me decide on that dress," I tell Claire as we get into my car. "I'm sure I never would've picked it out by myself."

"No problem. You know how much I love to shop." She leans back into the seat and sighs happily. "And it was fun doing something with you again. I thought you were going to blow me off for good."

As I start my car, I try to make it clear that I hope we can keep being friends. I feel like I'm stumbling over the words, and I'm sure she knows that I've had some reservations about hanging with her.

"I know that some of my friends think I've got problems," she says finally.

"Everyone has problems," I say quickly.

"Yeah, but I know the reason Haley and Stacy and Megan avoid me is because of my drinking. But honestly, I've been doing better lately. I think I've got it under control."

"Cool," I say as I exit the parking lot. Now I'm trying to think of some casual way to introduce the idea of possibly inviting Simi and Andrew to join us on prom night, but it's just not coming.

"Hey, wanna stop and get a bite to eat?" she asks as she points to a small, slightly rundown Italian restaurant down the street. "My treat, okay? My little thank-you for giving me a ride today."

"Sounds good," I admit. "I'm starving." When we get to the parking lot, I call home and tell my mom that I won't be home for dinner.

"Did you find a dress?" my mom asks in an interested voice. So I tell her about it and then explain about the tear, but she assures me she can fix it.

"Good for you for finding a bargain," she says. "Especially since you'll only need the dress for one night." *Just like Simi,* I'm thinking as I agree and then tell her goodbye.

Soon we are seated in the restaurant and the waitress is asking if we'd like something to drink.

"I'll have a Fuzzy Navel," says Claire, cool as ever.

Now, why am I not surprised by this? And yet I'm feeling irritated—seriously irritated. I give her a glance, but she is ignoring me.

"I'll have to see your ID," says the waitress, who looks to be about our age or slightly older.

Claire opens her Prada purse and whips out her fake ID. The waitress takes a quick look but seems satisfied.

"How about you?" she turns to me. "Can I get you anything?"

"Don't make me drink alone," says Claire in a pleading voice. "And remember, it's my treat tonight." She smiles up at the waitress. "I know, why don't you skip the Fuzzy Navel and just bring us a carafe of Merlot and an extra glass for my friend."

"I'll have to see your friend's ID first." The waitress looks at me and I feel my face heating with embarrassment. I decide that the quickest way to resolve this might simply be to show her my fake ID. So I fumble in my purse for the card, saying to Claire that I really don't want wine anyway.

"But you might change your mind," Claire says pleasantly as she turns back to the waitress. "We just did some serious shopping damage at Nordstrom's," she explains to the waitress. "I think we deserve a nice little break now."

I can't believe how well Claire can pull this stuff off. I hand my ID over to the waitress and wait for her to examine it and probably call the manager and have me thrown out, but she just nods and hands it to me, saying that she'll be right back with our wine.

"Claire," I hiss once the waitress is gone. "Why did you do that?"

"Why not?"

Soon there is a carafe of dark wine and two glasses at our table. I glance uncomfortably around the dimly lit restaurant, seriously worried that someone from my church might be here tonight. Fortunately, we're in a corner in the back and I don't recognize anyone. But by the time I focus my attention back to our table, I notice that

Claire has already filled my wine glass and is now holding hers up as if she wants to toast.

"To friendship," she says.

Feeling like a hypocritical fool, I stupidly lift my glass as I faintly echo her toast and then take a small obligatory sip. But I am determined that I will not take another one.

seventeen

I'M WONDERING IF I MAY HAVE SOME SERIOUS CHARACTER FLAW OR INNER weakness or if maybe I'm just plain stupid, because not only do I drink two glasses of wine with our dinner but afterward I let Claire talk me into heading to the bar that's attached to the restaurant.

"Not to drink," she assures me. "Just for fun."

I nod, trying to remember my earlier resolve. "All right, just for fun. Don't forget that I'm driving, okay?"

"Yeah, maybe you should have some coffee."

So we go to a booth against the wall. The place isn't very busy, but it takes the middle-aged cocktail waitress a while to come to our table.

"Are you kids old enough to be in here?" She frowns down on us with a skeptical expression.

Claire just laughs and reaches for her purse. As the woman checks Claire's ID, I fumble around for mine. Although I'm feeling more relaxed now, I still get uneasy as I hand over the fake ID. But the woman simply nods and hands it back.

"The older I get, the younger everyone else looks," she says as she flips open a small pad. "Now, what would you like?"

Claire, despite her promise not to drink, orders a Fuzzy Navel, but I say I just want coffee.

"You should try it with Baileys," suggests Claire.

"What's that?"

"Irish cream," says the woman. "It's pretty good."

"Okay," I agree. And since I'm still trying to acquire a taste for coffee, I think some Irish cream, whatever that is, might be good.

It's not long before she brings our drinks, and my coffee does taste pretty good. And it's not long before we both order a second round.

"Does Irish cream have alcohol in it?" I ask Claire as I take a sip from my second cup.

"A little."

I roll my eyes. "You know you could've told me that earlier."

"Well, don't worry, the caffeine in the coffee will probably balance it out."

And so I don't worry. In fact, I think I'm feeling pretty good as we watch some loser-type guys who seem to have their eye on us from the bar. Hopefully they won't offer to buy us drinks. Claire has assured me that she will get rid of them if they try to get friendly.

Finally I'm feeling relaxed enough to bring up the subject of Simi and Andrew. "Oh, yeah," I say as if I'd just thought of it. "I was meaning to ask you if a couple of friends could come to the prom with us."

"Who's that?"

"Simi and a guy from North. His name is Andrew something. He's really cute, and I'll bet he knows Eric."

She smiles. "Cool. The more the merrier."

And so, just like that, it's all arranged, and I'm wondering why I was so worried about it.

Just as I'm really starting to relax, a couple of women walk into the bar, and to my horrified amazement, one of the women looks exactly like Simi's older sister, Lena. In fact, it *is* Lena. But she doesn't see me as they go to the far end of the bar and sit down.

Now, I realize that Lena is old enough to be in here, but I also know that she's a Christian, and I'm feeling more than a little shocked to see her here. I don't recognize the woman she's with, but I can tell she's older than Lena, like maybe in her thirties. Fortunately, Lena hasn't noticed me yet. But I'm not sure how we're going to get out of here without being seen since both exits are clearly visible from where Lena and her friend are sitting.

I whisper this news to Claire, but she just thinks it's funny. "So what's the big deal?"

"Lena goes to my church."

"Well, then you're both just a couple of sinners, right?"

"Yeah, but I'm underage, not to mention the pastor's daughter. And Lena might tell someone."

She just shrugs and sips her drink. "She probably won't even see you. Besides, doesn't it make you feel better to know that someone from your church enjoys a drink or two occasionally? Lighten up, Amber."

I'm not sure what I think about that. To be honest, I find it disturbing that Lena drinks. For one thing, I always think of her as something of a role model, although I'd never admit that to anyone. But beyond that, Simi just said recently that Lena is going to be helping Glen with youth group this summer. In fact, Simi thinks that Lena and Glen might even sort of like each other.

So I'm confused. Like, what's up with this? I try to see what Lena is drinking, but it just looks like a regular Coke. Of course, I know full well that you can drink something that looks like an innocent Coke but isn't.

"Just chill," says Claire. "And quit staring at them, or you'll draw her attention for sure."

"Yeah." I sit sort of sideways now, just in case Lena turns around to look this way.

"Another round?" asks the cocktail waitress with a bored expression.

Naturally, Claire (who's been "cutting back," yeah right) orders another Fuzzy Navel, but I say that I've had enough—more than enough is what I'm thinking.

"Oh, bring her one too," says Claire in a slightly slurred voice. "Even if she just sits here and looks at it. I don't want to drink alone, you know?"

"You sure?" asks the woman, glancing at me now.

"Hey, the drinks are on me anyway," says Claire. "Go ahead and bring her another."

"I think we should go," I whisper after the waitress leaves.

"Why are you whispering?" asks Claire in a voice that's loud enough to be heard over the music that's blaring through the speaker just over our heads.

I glance uncomfortably at the bar but then feel relieved to see that Lena and her friend seem to be deep in conversation and not even looking our way.

So I take a deep breath and try to relax. And when the woman brings our drinks, I go ahead and take a tiny sip, telling myself that I'll just pretend to drink it until Lena and her friend leave, and then we can go too.

But I am halfway through my drink and actually feeling pretty good when I feel someone tapping me on the shoulder. I look up to see Lena looking down at me. Her face is a mixture of confusion and, I think, anger.

"What are you doing here, Amber?" she asks.

Of course, I can't think of anything to say. I just stare at her in shocked horror and wish I could disappear.

"Amber?" she continues. "Really, what on earth are you doing here?"

I hold up my half-full cup. "Having coffee," I say meekly.

She bends down and takes a sniff of my cup. "*Spiked* coffee."

I shrug.

"Who's your friend?" asks Lena as she slides in beside me.

"Uh, this is, uh—"

Claire makes a cute little wave with her pinkie finger and then smiles at Lena like she's seeing double.

"Never mind." Lena is reaching for my arm now, and before I can say anything, she has pulled me to my feet. "Let's go outside and talk, Amber."

I glance hopelessly at Claire, but she only looks highly amused by this unfortunate scene. The next thing I know, I'm standing outside in the dark parking lot with Lena looking down on me.

"What is up with this, Amber?" she demands.

"I don't know." I stare at the ground now, seriously wishing that it would open up and swallow me.

"Of all people, I cannot believe that you would do something like this—something so totally stupid."

And that's when my courage suddenly returns to me. Maybe it's the alcohol, or maybe I'm just fed up with everything, but now I'm ready to confront her. "How about you?" I begin in a defiant tone. "What are *you* doing here?"

Her face is only a few inches from mine now, and it actually looks rather frightening in the greenish light that comes from the neon sign above the entrance to the bar.

"For your information, little girl, I came here with a friend from the counseling center I work at. I've been trying to get her to come to church with me, and she told me that she would come to church if I would go to a bar with her to just talk—kind of a challenge, I guess. So I agreed to come, but only after I informed her that I would only drink a Coke."

"Oh."

"And furthermore, I am twenty-two and old enough to be in here legally, whereas you are not. How did you get in here anyway?"

"My feet?"

"Amber!" I swear I think she's growling now.

"Fake ID," I say in a quiet voice, hoping that maybe she won't hear me.

"Let's see it."

So I dig in my purse until I find the plastic card, and feeling like I'm about five years old and caught red-handed, I give it to her.

"Thanks." She sticks it in her purse.

"Hey—"

"Don't *hey* me," she says in the same tough voice that I've heard Simi use over the years when she's mad. "You're not getting it back. Don't even ask—ever!"

I shrug. "Yeah, well, that's probably a good thing."

Now she seems to soften just a little. "Seriously, Amber, what is up with this? I mean, I just don't get it. It's not like you. What's going on?"

"I don't know."

Now Claire is coming toward us, and I can tell by the way she's walking, kind of like a slithering snake only upright, that she's pretty smashed.

"Wha's going on out here?" she asks slowly as if she's having a hard time forming the words. "You girls gonna fight or somethin'?"

Lena looks totally exasperated now. "What's going on is that I'm calling you two a taxi and you're going straight home."

"What about my car?" I ask.

"Forget about it. You are *not* driving anywhere tonight, Amber Conrad. I cannot believe you would even consider— "

"I'm not drunk," I plead with her, even though I'm not so sure. "Really, Lena, I'm not drunk."

"Maybe not as drunk as your friend—what *is* your name anyway?" she demands.

"Claire," I answer quickly, not offering a last name just in case Lena is into calling parents tonight.

"Where are your car keys, Amber?"

"But I— "

"No buts, Amber—unless you want me to call your dad right now. And then I'll have to tell him where I found you and ask him to come pick you up." She is brandishing her cell phone like a weapon now, so I dig around in my purse until I find my keys and, feeling like the village idiot, hand them over.

Now Lena is dialing her cell phone, but it seems she's talking to information, and it's not long before she's connected to a cab company and giving them the restaurant's location. I feel totally helpless to do anything but stand there and watch as my life flashes before my eyes.

Claire is in her own world now, singing a stupid Eminem song that I can't even stand when I'm snookered—not that I am.

"I'd take you home myself, but I need to give Debbie a ride." She frowns. "Speaking of Debbie, I hate to have left her alone this long. We were actually having a really great conversation about forgiveness and grace."

"Barroom evangelism?" I say in my best sarcastic tone, the same line that Lena's little sister used on me not so long ago.

"Call it what you like, Amber, but at least I'm legal here, and *I'm* not drinking."

"Yeah, whatever."

"There's the cab now," she says. Then, taking us both by the arms, she walks us over and opens the door and instructs the driver to take us to our homes and then hands him some money.

I give him the address of Claire's house first, but when we get there, she begs me to come in with her. "Nobody's home," she says in a sad voice. "Why don' you come in and spend the night?"

I almost agree, but then I realize that Lena will probably be checking up on me before long. "Not tonight," I tell her.

"Next time," she says as she waves and walks in a zigzag to her front door.

I chew down several breath mints as the cab driver takes me home. I'm preparing myself for whatever might happen. I'm pretty sure there will be some kind of confrontation at my house.

But when I get home, I am pleasantly surprised to see that no one is there. There's a note from my parents saying that they've gone out for ice cream. Going out for ice cream is my parents' idea of a romantic date. I guess it goes back to the days when they were dating and penniless. Whatever. I'm just relieved they're not here yet.

I go to the bathroom and brush my teeth and splash cold water on my face. Then I go to the kitchen and make a strong pot of coffee. I figure that if I down a few cups, I just might be sober by the time the big confrontation occurs, because I feel certain that there will be one. It's just a matter of time.

It's almost nine when the phone rings, and I'm not terribly surprised to discover it's Lena.

"Glad to see you made it home, Amber."

"Yeah, thanks a lot."

"Are your parents around?"

"No, they went out for ice cream. I'm sure they'll be back soon."

"Well, I just got home and I was talking to Simi, and she's actually willing to drive your car home for you. I'm not even sure why."

"She'd do that for me?"

"Yes. But only if you let her spend the night tonight. And only if you and she can have a nice long talk."

"Sure," I say quickly. "That's cool."

So now I'm thinking that maybe my parents won't have to find out after all. Maybe I can make some kind of deal with Simi, or maybe I can make her understand how I feel, like how frustrated I am and how I never intended to go out drinking tonight.

eighteen

Simi is totally amazing. Not only is she understanding and sympathetic when I tell her that I didn't want things to go like this tonight, but she says that she and Lena won't tell my parents. Then when my parents get home, she chats pleasantly with them for a few minutes, and I show my mom my prom dress. And I can tell they think life is perfectly normal.

Then Simi and I go back in my room and she tells me there are certain conditions. "You only get this second chance," she begins, "if you quit this stupidity right now. Lena and I discussed it, and we think it's fair. And we mean it, Amber. You have to get your life back on track."

"What if I can't?"

"Then we're going to rat on you."

"Is this some kind of blackmail?"

She shrugs. "No. Just consider it another form of peer pressure." Then she puts her hand on my arm. "Seriously, Amber, we just want you to be healthy, to quit this moronic drinking and partying and stuff—and to get your heart right with the Lord. That's all."

I'm crying now. "That's what I want too."

"Really?"

I nod. And this is the truth. I *do* want it. I'm just not sure how to get it. "I just don't know if I can really do it."

"What do you mean?"

"I mean I'm worried that something's wrong with me, Simi." I look straight into her face. "It's like I'm such a wimp, or maybe I'm flawed, or—" I choke on a sob. "Maybe I'm really an alcoholic."

She looks unconvinced. "I don't think you can become an alcoholic in just a few weeks, Amber."

"How do you know?"

She shrugs. "I guess I don't."

"Well, I read something online. It was written by a girl who started drinking when she was my age, and she said that she knew she was an alcoholic when she took her first drink. She didn't get over it until she was about thirty." I'm crying hard now. "And it really—really wrecked her life and she was so—so messed up and—what—what if that's me?"

Simi hugs me now. "We won't let that be you, Amber. You've got friends and family—people who love you and who want to help. We won't let you end up like that."

"But—but—from everything I've read—I know that only the alcoholic can change herself. Other people can't do it for her."

"But we can stand by you, Amber. Hey, I'd even go to an Alcoholics Anonymous meeting with you if it would help."

I sit up straighter now. "You think I need to go to an AA meeting?"

"I don't know. Whatever it takes."

I feel like someone has just poured a bucket of ice water over my head. "I don't need to go to AA," I say in a firm voice. "I'm not an alcoholic."

"You're the one who said that—"

"Well, I was just talking," I say.

“Then why did you do all that research?” she challenges.

“I was worried about Claire.”

Simi nods. “You should be. I honestly think she *is* an alcoholic.”

I don’t say anything.

“And maybe you’re not, Amber. Maybe you’ve just been making some stupid choices.”

I nod. “Yeah. Really stupid.”

“Do you think you can quit drinking?”

I nod again. “Yeah. I’m sure I can.”

“So, do you promise you won’t drink again?”

I consider this. Despite how much I’ve blown it lately, I’m a person who takes a promise seriously. I don’t like making any that I can’t keep.

“We need your word on this, Amber.”

“I want to promise,” I begin, “but I’m not sure.”

“So you really think you’re not done with this thing?”

“Can I be really honest with you, Simi?”

“That’s the goal here.”

“Okay. The truth is, I don’t want to drink again—really, I hate the feeling of losing control. I hate getting sick, and it scares me to death when I realize that I’ve driven under the influence.”

“You’ve done that?”

I swallow and look down at my lap. “Yeah, and trust me, I’m not proud of it.”

“You could kill someone, Amber.”

“I know.”

“But I don’t get it.”

I look back at her. “What?”

“If it’s so awful, like you just said, then why do you keep doing it? It doesn’t make sense.”

"I know. It doesn't make sense to me either. The only thing I can tell you is that I like how it makes me feel—at the beginning anyway. Having a drink or two just loosens me up and I start to act more normal. I mean, you don't know how hard it is for me. You're so comfortable with yourself, but *I* always have to push myself to act normal, to talk to people, to get out of my little shell."

"What makes you think I'm not doing the same thing?" she challenges me.

"Because you're naturally outgoing."

"Not as much as you think. I have to push myself too, Amber. Everyone is a little insecure about something, but getting drunk isn't going to fix that."

"No, I guess not."

"But you're still not convinced?"

I shrug and look away.

"Okay, let me ask you this, Amber. Remember a week or so ago when your dad preached about how we know if something is sin or not?"

"Not exactly."

"Yeah, you probably had a hangover that day."

Even though it's probably true, I act offended.

"Anyway, he said we should ask ourselves something."

"That would be?"

"We should ask ourselves if the questionable activity makes us feel closer to God. Does drinking alcohol make you feel closer to God?"

I consider this but don't answer.

"Well, does it?"

I shake my head. "If anything, it's made me feel further and further away from God."

"So you'd have to agree that it's sin."

"Yeah."

"So why would you keep doing it?"

"Because I'm weak. I'm a loser. I'm hopeless, pathetic—you name it."

"That's not true," she tells me. "I've known you for years, and you were never any of those things—well, not until you started drinking. Then you turned into someone else."

I sigh. "I'm tired of being that person."

"Are you sure?"

"I think I am. But I'm just trying to be honest. I'm still worried that I'll fall back into it, like I told you about tonight. I had no intention of—"

"Well, you should probably stay away from Claire. I mean, have you ever done anything with her that didn't involve alcohol?"

"Yeah—well, at least on my part. I think she pretty much drinks all the time."

"See, she's not a good influence."

"No. But I think she needs a good influence."

"And you think you've been one?"

"Not really."

"Well, if you want to spend any time with Claire, maybe you should have someone like me along."

That reminds me of the prom plans, so I tell her.

"That's a good start. But I'll only agree to go with you guys if you can keep it together this week. You think you can do that?"

"I'll try."

"And I expect you to be honest with me, Amber."

"I will."

Then she asks me to try on my prom dress for her to see, and I do, and after that we act like our old normal selves. We talk about boys and clothes, and she tries putting my hair up in a style she thinks would look good on prom night. And I'm thinking, *Yeah, this is what it's supposed to be like.*

We go to church together the next morning, but I have to slip out early to get to work. Simi gives me a look that says, "Remember your promise." And I nod.

The week goes pretty smoothly, and when Claire asks me to go to lunch at Merenda's on Wednesday, I tell her that I've already promised to have lunch with Simi.

"Well, bring her along," says Claire. "My treat."

So I invite Simi and am totally shocked when she agrees to come. When I question her about breaking the rules of closed campus, she just tells me to lighten up. "Even Jesus broke the rules sometimes," she says. "Remember how the priests called him a Sabbath breaker?"

Then I warn Simi about Claire's need to imbibe at lunch, but she acts like it's no big deal.

"So you won't like freak or anything?" I question.

"I just want to get to know her better," she says.

And so the three of us are walking to Merenda's together. We're talking about the prom, and Simi describes her dress, and Claire seems to approve.

"I'll bet you look really striking in red," says Claire as we reach the deli counter. "It just completely washes me out."

Now, I haven't told Claire about my confiscated ID yet. But true to tradition, she orders wine. And since the woman at the register has seen us before, she doesn't even ask for ID.

"What's up with that?" asks Simi as she and I head for a table. "She didn't even card her."

I quickly explain, and then Claire joins us.

"Is it going to bother you that I'm having wine?" asks Claire with the most innocent-looking blue eyes.

Simi shrugs. "I don't think it's a good idea personally, but I guess it's your choice."

Claire nods.

Then Simi leans forward and looks directly at Claire. "But I have to ask you something, if you don't mind."

"Ask away."

"Well, I'm just curious as to why you need to drink. Do you know why you do it?"

"Because I want to."

"What would happen if you didn't drink?"

"I'd feel lousy."

"How do you feel when you drink?"

Claire seems to consider this. "To be honest, I don't feel anything at all."

"And that's good?"

"It's good for me."

"So you're trying to escape your feelings?"

Claire frowns. "What are you, like some kind of shrink?"

"Sorry," says Simi.

Then the conversation pauses as the woman sets our order on the table. Claire goes straight for her wine, taking a long drink before she turns back to Simi.

"So why are you so interested in my drinking habits, Simi?"

"I'm just curious. It just seems like you're throwing a lot away."

"And that would be?"

"Your life. I mean, if you spend all your time getting drunk just to escape your feelings, well, you can't be having much of a life."

Claire is silent as she downs the rest of her wine.

"And you seem like an interesting person," continues Simi. "But it's like you're just throwing it all away."

"That's your perspective." Claire is glancing over to the counter, and I can tell she's hoping that someone will come over and see if we need something, since I suspect she's wanting another glass of wine. But no one comes.

"And do you know what I think?" says Simi as she sets down her fork.

"No, but I'm sure I'm going to hear about it anyway."

Simi smiles. "Just this last thing, and then I'll stop, okay?"

"Deal."

"I think you're running from your emotions because they make you feel weak and helpless. But the reason you feel weak and helpless is because deep down you know you need God in your life."

Claire's eyes are wide, and it almost looks like she's about to start crying. Instead, she waves to the woman behind the counter and, pointing to her empty glass, says, "I'll have another."

So that's pretty much the end of Simi's little outreach session, but I have to admit that I'm impressed. Claire doesn't say much after that. But Simi and I manage to make enough small talk to keep things from feeling too heavy.

Later on that day, when Simi and I are both at work, I ask her about her questions to Claire.

"How did you know to ask those things?" I ask.

"I don't know. It's like it was a God thing." She shakes her head. "I mean, it just came to me, but it felt so right."

"I've never seen Claire get so uncomfortable about anything before. It's like you were really getting to her."

"Cool."

"I guess."

"I hope she doesn't decide that she doesn't want Andrew and me to go to the prom with you guys now."

"I don't think that'll happen." I rearrange the drink cups. "If anything, I think she really wants to get to know you better now. She called my cell when I was on the way over here and asked me some things about you."

"Like what?"

"I don't know. But I can tell she wants to get to know you better." I kind of laugh. "Maybe you can take my place with her."

"Well, except for the drinking." She gives me an elbow.

And I can take her teasing today. I mean, so far this week has gone really well for me. I haven't had one drink and I haven't even been tempted. Even so, I'm not sure that I'm done with it yet. And I have to admit that prom night is looming before me like a huge test that I'm afraid I'll fail—and not only will I fail but I'll fail right in front of Simi. And then what?

I know I should take Simi's advice and get my heart right before God, but it's like I don't want to do it until *after* the prom. Now, how lame is that? But it's the truth.

nineteen

So just when I'm thinking maybe I have control over this thing, I totally mess up. It's Friday, just one day before prom night, and to be honest, I'm feeling a little uptight. In fact, I even admitted this much to Slater on the phone this afternoon. (I'd called him from work to see how his track meet had gone—not well, unfortunately.)

"I know what you mean," he told me after I confessed to feeling on edge about the prom. "It's like everyone's acting like it's such a big freaking deal. I don't get it. It's just a stupid dance."

"I know," I said.

"How about I stop by for your dinner break tonight?" he asks. "Maybe I can help you loosen up."

"Sure," I tell him. "That'd be cool."

So Slater shows up at six, and I tell Simi that I'll be back in half an hour so she can take her break. But what I don't know is that Slater has brought a libation to pour into our sodas. "Just something to loosen you up," he teases as he sneaks some rum into my Dr Pepper.

I know it's wrong, and I feel totally horrible and guilty and foolish, but I give in and drink it anyway. The whole time I'm telling myself that I'm an idiot.

"It's not like we're getting wasted," Slater assures me. "And I'm not going to give you any more. It's just to loosen up, you know, to relax and have fun."

Well, we get so relaxed that we start acting pretty goofy, and before I know it, it's after seven. "Oh, no," I tell him. "I'm really late. I gotta go."

So he walks me back to The Caramel Corn Shoppe and kisses me goodbye. Then I have to go and explain to Simi.

"It's okay," she says.

"But I'm so sorry," I tell her, almost crying. "I didn't mean to stay so long. I'm so stupid. I wasn't—"

"Amber?" She's holding on to my shoulders now and looking right into my eyes. "Have you been drinking?"

I do start crying now, but determined to continue my stupidity, I deny it. "No," I tell her. "I just had a Dr Pepper with my dinner." But I know she's not buying it.

"Don't lie, Amber."

I glance around the shop, wishing a customer would come in and interrupt us, but it's just not happening. "I just had one little tiny drink," I finally tell her. "Slater put it in my soda. I didn't mean to—"

"You broke your promise."

"But I—"

"You broke your promise."

"I didn't mean—"

"Let me ask you something, Amber," she interrupts me, "and give me an honest answer, okay?"

"Okay."

"Do you control your drinking, or does your drinking control you?"

To my relief, customers come now—a whole herd of them. It's a couple of moms and about six kids between the two of them, and I somehow get myself together enough to be useful. After what seems like about twenty minutes, they are finally gone.

"Why don't you take your dinner break now," I suggest, avoiding Simi's eyes and hoping to escape her previous question.

She takes off her apron, hangs it up, and walks out without saying a word. Okay, that makes me feel worse than anything, but I tell myself it's no big deal. I mean, Simi's a Christian. She has to forgive me, right?

I hear a ringing sound from underneath the counter and realize it's my cell. When I answer it, it's Claire, and she's upset.

"It's my moronic stepdad," she says in a hysterical voice. "He's making me crazy."

"Calm down," I tell her. "What's wrong?"

"He says I'm grounded, that I can't go to the prom. And I'm so—so—" And then she starts sobbing.

"Take it easy," I say. "Take a deep breath."

So she talks some more and begs me to meet her somewhere.

"As long as it's not a bar," I warn her. "How about Starbucks over by the mall where I work?"

So it's agreed that we'll meet after I get off.

Simi comes back in exactly thirty minutes, almost as if to rub it in. But she's still not saying anything. We continue on like that for the next hour, and finally it's closing time and we go through the paces like two robots. No words, no visible emotions—just mechanical motions. Then it's all locked up and we're walking across the parking lot toward our cars and I just can't take it anymore.

"Okay!" I yell at Simi. "I'm a loser. I know it. I'm a total failure. I'm hopeless. But I told you this last week. I told you that I think I have a problem."

She turns and looks at me. "Are you an alcoholic?"

"No," I say quickly. "I just have a problem."

"Oh."

"But I won't do it again, Simi," I tell her. "Honestly, I don't want to be like this, and I don't want us to be like this. I'm going to quit—really."

"*Going* to?"

"Okay. I quit. I'm done. *Finis*."

She just sighs and shrugs. "Yeah, whatever."

"So, are we okay then?" I ask.

"Yeah." Then she reaches out and suddenly hugs me. "It's just that I worry about you, Amber. It's only because I love you, you know?"

"I know."

Then she steps back and looks at me. "And you're okay to drive home? I could give you a ride, but I have to stop by and pick up Lena first. Her car's in the shop."

"That's okay. I'll be fine. Really, it was just one shot of rum in my Dr Pepper, and it was with food. Not enough to impair anyone."

"Well, drive carefully anyway."

I nod again. But it's like there's this big lump forming in my throat right now, like I'm about to cry, but I really don't want her to see me falling apart.

"You too," I call out as she gets into her car.

Then I get into my car and wait for her to leave. Then I just slam my fist into my steering wheel and let loose with a scream that's coming from some deep dark place inside me. Why am I such a mess? Why can't I get this right? I yell at myself for a couple minutes and then suddenly remember my promise to meet Claire. Sometimes my life exhausts me.

I exit the mall and drive down the street, and just as I'm wondering about what's going on with Claire, I see flashing red and blue lights coming from behind me. I check my speedometer, but I'm barely going thirty. Even so, I pull over. As I do, I'm aware that I am driving under the influence, and I wonder how much one shot of rum will register on a breathalyzer test. Yet it's almost as if I don't care. Maybe this is what it will take to make me stop.

But the police car just whizzes past me with siren blaring and lights flashing. Feeling like I've dodged a bullet, I carefully pull back onto the street. As I approach the traffic lights, I see that the police car has stopped at the intersection, and there's another one just pulling up from the other direction. As I get closer, I see that there's been a wreck.

What appears to be a silver Mercedes is sitting diagonally at a corner of the intersection. All of a sudden I remember that Claire sometimes drives her mom's silver Mercedes! I stop my car on the side of the street and, leaving the engine running, jump out and run over.

"Stay back," says an officer.

"But I know her," I say.

"Who?"

"The driver of the Mercedes!" I point to the silver car where two police officers are opening the passenger door and looking inside.

"That's my friend!" I yell at the officer as I push past him and run toward the car. *"Claire!"* I scream as I see her with her head bent over and an exploded air bag spread across her lap. But then she opens her eyes and looks at me. She is stunned, but she seems to be okay. And the policemen are asking if she can move. She says yes, and I feel a rush of relief. That's when I stand up to see what it is she's hit—or what's left of it.

"That Mercedes ran the red light and T-boned the Volkswagen!" a man is telling a policeman. "Must've been going at least forty-five miles an hour too."

I can tell by the rear of the car, the only part that's still partially intact, that it's not just a Volkswagen but also a Bug. And then I realize it's an *orange* Bug—just like the one Simi drives. And I remember that she had left just ahead of me. My heart stops.

"Simi!" I scream into the night. I rush past Claire's car and over to the one that's been hit, but one of the policemen grabs me now. "You need to stay back," he says firmly. "It could catch fire!"

"But that's my friend!" I'm screaming at the top of my lungs. "That's *Simi Gartolini*, my best friend. I *have* to see her!"

"Stay back, young lady. They need to get the driver out of the car before—"

"Simi!" I scream as he holds me back.

Other vehicles with flashing lights and sirens are coming down the street toward us now, and soon they are prying open the passenger's door and extracting Simi from the crumpled car. I can see them putting her on a stretcher. In that same moment, the officer who's been detaining me becomes distracted and I break free and run over and stand behind the paramedics, peering over their shoulders to see if it's really my best friend. I gasp when I see her. I have no doubt that it's Simi now. I recognize her dark ponytail, still pulled back into the white barrette she always uses for work. But that's about all that's recognizable. Simi looks as twisted and broken as her little car, which is now starting to smoke.

"Everyone, get clear!" yells a fireman.

"Simi!" I scream, feeling my legs buckling beneath me, and everything begins to get blurry and then dark.

***

When I regain consciousness, I look up to see the same policeman that I ran from standing over me now. "Are you okay, miss?"

"Where's Simi?" I sit up and look across the street to the wreck site only to see firefighters hosing down what I assume was once Simi's little Bug, now reduced to a smoldering heap—a sad little pile of burnt orange.

"They're both in transit to Ashton General," he tells me. "They should be arriving about now."

"I've got to go," I tell him as I get to my feet.

"I don't think you should be driving so soon after passing out," he warns me.

"But I have to go." I look for my car and then see that it's been moved out of the way and onto a side street.

He hands me my keys. "Your car is fine there for the time being. We'll drive you to the hospital."

I sit silently in the back of the patrol car as we fly down the street with lights flashing.

"They were *both* your friends?" asks the policeman in the passenger's seat.

"Yes."

And then he asks me their names. I give not only their names but their phone numbers and parents' names as well.

"That's helpful," says the policeman, and I hear him radioing this information to someone somewhere. And in my head, I am praying. It's like some old spiritual instinct just kicked itself into gear, almost like I don't even have to think about it, and I can tell that I'm praying with my whole heart. I'm asking God to watch over Simi—and Claire too. I know it's the first time I've prayed in quite a while, yet it feels completely normal.

And then we're at the hospital. The police drop me at the emergency entrance, and I see the two ambulances by the door, engines running, lights still flashing, and the rear door on one of them still gaping open. And I can see splatters of blood on the floor in there and a guy who appears to be wiping it up, but it's like there is blood everywhere.

"Just let her be okay, God," I continue praying as I rush into the hospital. "Let them both be okay."

The receptionist informs me that both victims have been admitted but that it might be a while before we know anything. She questions me on their names and phone numbers again, and I give them to her. Then I just stand there staring at the clock over her head until she suggests I go sit down in the waiting area, and so I sit down and continue to pray. I feel like I'm praying with every ounce of spiritual energy I possess, and I'm amazed that I have any. Then after a while, it occurs to me that I have a responsibility to make my heart right before God. I mean, how can I sit here begging him to fix everything when I've been living like a complete jerk?

So I confess to God that I've blown it—blown it big-time. I confess that I've pushed him away and that I've chosen to live out my own Stupidity with a capital S. I tell him that I'm sorry—really and truly sorry—and that I'm done with all that crud, honestly and totally done. And I know this is the truth, and I know that he forgives me. I know it because it's what I've been taught for as long as I can remember. *If I confess my sins, he forgives my sins.* I know that Jesus died so that my sins could be washed away. All I need to do is to ask.

Okay, I know this in my head, but I have to admit that my heart is still wavering a little, yet I want to believe this wholeheartedly.

But I try not to think about that right now. Right now, all I want to do is ask God—beg him—to please, please, please spare my friends tonight. Okay, I know that I'm mostly praying for Simi right now. It's not that I'm not concerned about Claire. I am, but she didn't seem to be as badly hurt as Simi. Not only that, but I have a strong feeling that Claire is to blame for this whole thing. I feel certain that she was driving while intoxicated, and that is probably why she slammed into Simi's car tonight.

But somehow I feel that it's my fault as well, even though I can't put my finger on exactly why. But it is killing me. *Oh, God, I am soooo sorry.*

twenty

My best friend died tonight. I've just heard the news. She died on the way to the hospital. The paramedics tried to revive her, but her injuries were just too severe. She was literally crushed by Claire's car.

I wish it had been me instead.

I was with her parents and Lena when we heard the news. My parents were there too. Everyone fell completely apart. Simi's dad is blaming himself for allowing Simi to drive his old Volkswagen Bug. I am silently blaming Claire.

Claire's mom and stepdad are with Claire now. It seems that she only had minor injuries and is going to be okay. No one has mentioned alcohol yet, but Lena gave me a look, and I know that she knows. I think it's just a matter of time until everyone knows.

We're on our way to the hospital chapel now. My dad has taken over the official role of pastor, and he herds us like the hurting sheep we are. We huddle together in the small space. No one speaks, and finally my dad begins to pray.

"Dear heavenly Father," he says in a voice that's breaking, "we don't know why this happened tonight, we don't know why you decided to take Simi home with you, but we do know that's where she is right now. And as much as we love and miss her, we take comfort in knowing she is in your arms."

I can't hear or process the rest of his prayer. I am crying too hard. In fact, I'm making so much noise that I decide to leave the room. I go to the bathroom and lock myself in a stall and continue to bawl. It feels like my heart is literally breaking, like my chest is splitting open and all my guts are about to come pouring out. I wonder if Simi hurt this badly tonight.

I try to take comfort in my dad's words, and I really do believe they're true. I do believe that Simi is in heaven—that she's gone straight into the arms of Jesus—but I still feel horrible. I feel that I've lost my best friend, which is true, but worse than that, I feel that it's partly my fault. I feel that I could've done something to prevent it. That's what's killing me.

"Amber?"

I open the stall door and peer out to see Lena standing by the sink. "Are you all right?"

I step out and shake my head no and then start blubbering again. Lena is crying too, and I almost expect her to lay into me now, to yell at me and accuse me of being partially to blame for Simi's death. But she just opens her arms, and I fall into them.

"It's not your fault, Amber," she tells me in a voice choked with tears. "I know that you think it is, but it's not."

"But—but why?" I sob. "Why?"

"We may never know completely why," she says, "but like your dad said, we can trust that God didn't make a mistake tonight. And Simi is with him."

"But—what about Claire?" I step back now and watch Lena's face. "I'm certain she was driving under the influence."

Lena just nods.

"And she caused the wreck."

"I know."

"But what you don't know," I continue, determined to tell someone—anyone—the truth, "is that this is partly my fault too. Claire was driving to meet me. We were going to meet at Starbuck's to talk. She was upset about her stepdad—and—" But I fall apart again, unable to finish.

"That still doesn't make it your fault." She puts her hand on my shoulder.

"But I should've told Claire not to drive. I should've known that she'd been drinking."

"And you think she would've listened?"

"I don't know." Then I realize something else. "But it was my idea to meet at Starbucks," I say. "If I hadn't picked Starbucks—"

"Oh, Amber," says Lena, "we can all think of reasons to blame ourselves. My dad is blaming himself tonight because of the Volkswagen thing. My mom thinks it's her fault for allowing Simi to take a job where she worked at night. I feel guilty she was coming to pick me up."

I wipe my nose on a paper towel and take in a ragged breath. "I know," I say. "I understand how everyone feels guilty. But I think that besides Claire, I am most to blame."

"Then you better take your guilt to the cross, Amber, because that's why Jesus died. Remember?"

I nod.

"Simi dearly loved you, Amber, and she'd feel awful to see you torturing yourself like this tonight. Don't you realize that you're the main reason that Simi came to the Lord? When you started taking her to church back in middle school, her life turned completely around. And then Simi shared her faith with our parents and then with me. And, well, I think we can all be thankful to you for that."

I just look down at the floor. "But I miss her."

Lena has tears streaming down her face now. "Yeah, we all do."

We hug again, and I thank her. I feel a tiny bit better, but there's this deep, awful ache inside me. It's like a dull knife that twists and turns, and I don't think it will ever go away.

twenty-one

THE NEXT COUPLE OF DAYS ARE NOTHING MORE THAN A PAINFUL BLUR. I am like the walking dead. My parents try to comfort me, and Lena has called to check on me a couple of times. Of course, I didn't go to the prom on Saturday, and I think I may have scared Slater away for good—but then that was my intent.

Mostly I just want to be alone. I need this time to work out my issues with God. But I'm not mad at him—I'm mad at me. I cannot believe what a stupid fool I've been. But for Simi's sake, I am trying to forgive myself. Lena says that's what Simi would want.

"That's what she wanted when she was alive," Lena told me on the phone this morning. "For you to get your heart right with God and make better choices. And she must want that even more now." And I am trying. But I do have a major obstacle: Claire. I haven't spoken to her since the wreck, and I don't know if I can forgive her—ever. It's come out into the open that she was driving under the influence. Big surprise. Her blood alcohol level was .13, which is legally drunk. Charges are being pressed.

But as angry as I am at her, I realize that I could've easily been in her shoes. There were lots of times when I set myself up to kill someone while I was behind the wheel. So did Slater, so do thousands of kids—every single day. I just read that more than seventeen thousand people were killed in alcohol-related crashes last year, and around five hundred thousand are injured annually—and a lot of these accidents are caused by drivers in my age-group. Sobering facts.

Speaking of sobering, I had to confess something yesterday—not to a human but to God. I had to tell God that I've been more tempted to drink these last few days than ever before. But I know I can't admit this to anyone else, because I know that most people would not get it, especially in light of Simi's death.

But I do understand why I'm so tempted. It's because I want to escape. I don't want to feel anything anymore. I want to numb the endless pain of living with my stupid mistakes. I remember when Simi questioned Claire specifically about this at lunch that day, and I didn't quite get it at the time. I mean, I couldn't understand why anyone would want to stop *feeling* things. *Now I know.*

It's not until after Simi's funeral that I come clean with my parents. I tell them about how much I was drinking and sneaking around and the fake ID and everything. They are shocked, but they are also forgiving and supportive. Just the same, this is probably the end of my college scholarship. As Dad pointed out, the church will not want to sponsor a student with a drinking problem. I told him that I thought it should go to someone more deserving—maybe Lisa Chan. I think I'll be lucky to get in at the local community college, if I go at all. And right now I don't think I really care.

Then I call Lena and ask her if I should talk to her parents as well, to confess my involvement with Claire and how badly I've blown it lately, but she tells me no. She says it would only increase their pain. "It's enough that I know about it," she tells me. "At least for now."

"But I feel like I need to do something else," I tell her. "Something to make things better or right or maybe just less painful."

And that's when she asks me if I'd like to come to the counseling center and get some help, so I agree. I'm not sure how it will help, but I'm willing to do it for Lena—and for Simi.

***

Two weeks have passed since Simi died, and I think I am slowly getting better. But it's not easy. It's like the old two-steps-forward-and-one-step-back routine, or sometimes the other way around. Lena keeps telling me that in order to heal, I need to forgive Claire, but it's like I don't want to hear that. It's like my heart cannot process it—until today. Today Lena got through to me.

"Can't you see you're hurting Simi?" she said.

"How can that be?" I ask. "Claire caused Simi's death."

"You told me yourself that Simi had tried to reach out to Claire, that she'd agreed to go to the prom with you guys just so that she could try to help her. And now you have a chance to make Simi's death count for something. You could reach out to Claire for Simi's sake."

And so I call Claire today. I've already heard the news—that she's been charged with vehicular manslaughter and driving under the influence. And after being arrested and held briefly, she is now out on bail, but her trial is scheduled for later this summer. Naturally, it's been the talk of the school, and naturally, Claire no longer attends—nor will she graduate with us next week.

It is extremely awkward to talk to Claire, but I am doing it for Simi. After some initial stilted conversation, she cuts to the chase.

"I thought you probably hated me," she says in a voice that's just as dead as my own.

"I sort of did."

"Did?"

I sigh. "Okay, I'm trying, for Simi's sake, to forgive you."

"Oh."

"I know that's what Simi would want."

Now Claire begins to quietly cry.

"Simi actually cared about you," I tell her. "She knew you had a serious problem and that you needed help." I clear my throat. "She had the same concerns for me."

"But I suppose *your* drinking days are over now."

"I hope so." And then I realize that if this is going to work, if I really want to reach this girl, I have to be honest. And so I confess to her that every single day and every single night, I have wanted a drink.

"Not just a drink," I admit, "but I want to get so wasted that I don't feel anything—not a thing."

"Really?"

"But I'm not going to do it," I say with fresh resolve.

"How?" she asks me. "How can you be that strong?"

"It's not me," I say. "It's God in me. Every day I tell him that I'm weak, that I want a drink, and I ask him to help me. And every day he does."

"Oh."

But I think I hear this ever-so-faint sense of longing in that *oh,* so I decide to take this thing one step further. "But I'm still worried," I tell her. "I think I may need more help."

"What do you mean?"

"I'm thinking about going to Alcoholics Anonymous."

"Seriously?"

Now I pray about this next thing, and I get the strongest sense that Simi is standing right next to me now, that she's right here urging me to say this.

"Do you think you'd want to come with me?" I ask.

There's a long pause, and I almost wonder if she hung up on me, but then she speaks. "Yeah, I think that'd be a good thing."

And so it's settled. I tell my parents and Lena about what I'm going to do, and they all seem to agree that it's a good idea. To be honest, I'm not so sure. For one thing, I don't know if I'm ready to be around Claire again, but at the same time, I do have this sense of peace. And strange as it sounds, I get this feeling that Simi is in it with me, like she's right here encouraging me to go through with it.

And so I go to Claire's house on the following Tuesday evening just a little before seven. Her mother answers the door and is obviously aware of what's going on tonight. But she says little to me and just calls for Claire to come and then leaves.

I am shocked when I see Claire. She looks like a different person. Her blonde hair is pulled back into a limp ponytail, and even though she's wearing a baggy set of pale gray sweats, I can see that she's lost weight. And she has dark shadows beneath her eyes and not a trace of makeup on her pale face. It's like she's someone else, or a ghost.

We are both quiet as I drive to the church where the AA meeting is being held, but as I drive, I silently pray—for both of us. For the first time, it occurs to me that Claire and I may have lost more than Simi did that night. I mean, as much as I miss her, Simi is with God. She is at peace and perfectly happy, yet Claire and I are still trying to pick up the pieces of our totally messed-up lives—Claire, I think, even more so than me, now that I've seen her.

We sit in the back of the room, watching as people of all ages and descriptions go forward and share their stories. Each story is different and yet so similar that it's almost comforting, or perhaps frightening.

And then it's my turn to go up. With sweaty palms, I walk to the front of the room. And here's the honest truth: more than ever, I would love a stiff drink right now—something to bolster me and give that sense of confidence that I so desperately lack. But more than that *I want God in my life*, and I want to live the kind of life that will make my dear friend Simi proud of me. And so I stand at the wooden podium and take in a deep breath and begin.

"Hello." I hear the shakiness in my voice. "My name is Amber Conrad, and I'm an alcoholic."

reader's guide

1. Why do you think Amber decided to go to a drinking party in the first place? Why did she decide to go again?
2. Do you think Amber's relationship with God was genuine? Why or why not?
3. Amber told herself that she "just wanted to have fun." Do you think she really had fun?
4. Do you think peer pressure affected Amber? How does it affect you?
5. Could Amber's Christian friends have done anything different to help her? What would you do if your friend were to start drinking?
6. Why do you think there are laws prohibiting minors from drinking alcohol?
7. Amber tried to convince herself that she was helping Claire. Do you think Claire benefited from Amber's friendship? Why or why not?
8. Lena put Amber and Claire into a cab to keep them from driving while intoxicated. What would you do if your friend planned to drive while under the influence of alcohol?

9. How long do you think it takes to become an alcoholic? Can it happen to anyone? Could it happen to you or someone you love?
10. What would you do if you or someone you knew had a drinking problem?

Resources for more help and information on alcoholism:

Al-Anon: 1-888-4AL-ANON, www.al-anon.alateen.org
Focus Adolescent Services: 1-877-362-8727, www.focusas.com/Alcohol.html
American Council on Alcoholism: 1-800-527-5344
Alcoholics Anonymous: www.alcoholics-anonymous.org

TrueColors Book 6:

Fool's Gold

Coming in July 2005

The story of a "simple" girl who gets caught up in the "glamour" of the material world—and finds out how much it really costs.

One

MY COUSIN VANESSA THINKS SHOPPING IS A COMPETITIVE SPORT. HONestly, this chick could go for gold if the Olympic committee ever figured out how physically demanding clothes shopping really is. I was so puffed that I thought I was about to die at the mall this afternoon. And I'm a missionary kid (otherwise known as an MK) who can walk about the Papua New Guinean bush for kilometers without whinging—well, not much anyway.

But Vanessa was a force to be reckoned with today, with her Gucci shoes and plastic Prada purse (loaded with her daddy's plastic cards) as well as her accumulation of brightly colored shopping bags that she steadily collected until she passed some off to me to lug for her. Finally I realized that this girl was not about to give up until she found the "perfect" T-shirt. And she seemed to have something quite specific in mind, since I showed her dozens that I thought were adequate. But she was driven. In fact, she reminded me of that ridiculous bunny rabbit that used to be on a telly commercial—the one for the batteries that just kept going and going and going. And Vanessa was even wearing pink too. Finally I told my cousin I was zonked and asked if she minded if I grabbed a lemon squash in the food court until she finished up.

"A lemon what?" she asked.

"You know, a lolly water, soda pop, whatever you Yanks call it. I just need a break is all."

"You're not *tired*, are you?" Her wide blue eyes looked incredulous, almost as if she thought I had a few kangaroos loose in the top paddock, although I was thinking the same thing about her.

I nodded. "Yeah, I reckon I am. Do you mind terribly?"

She smiled. "I just love it when you say 'reckon' and 'terribly' and 'lolly water.' You sound like such a little Aussie."

As usual, that embarrassed me. "I can't help how I talk, Vanessa," I explained for about the twentieth time. "That's how everyone talks at my school in New Guinea. The accent tends to rub off when all your mates are from down under. Trust me, my mum is always correcting my English."

"Well, I think it's adorable, Hannah, but I can't believe you're flaking out on me already. The only reason I brought you along today was because I thought you could use a little—well, you know—*help*." The way she said the word "help," you'd have thought she was offering me a kidney transplant or something. Then she glanced at my outfit, taking in my faded-logo T-shirt, baggy cargo pants with a hole in one knee, and ancient rubber flip-flops that were once purple but now looked more like the color of old beets. "I mean, those clothes are okay for the jungle or working in the yard," she continued, "but you don't really want to go around LA looking like, well, like a missionary kid."

I rolled my eyes. "That's *like* what I am, Vanessa." I tried not to show my pride at picking up this Yankee slang word "like." It's *like* they use it as a verb and an adverb and just about any other sort of word. It's *like* this and *like* that. And I've, *like,* been trying to insert it here and there just so I'll fit in better with the Yanks.

"I *know* you're a missionary kid," she continued, "but you don't have to go around advertising the fact to everyone—I mean, unless you want people to feel sorry for you and you plan to pass the cup around like your dad does when he goes to churches to raise his mission money."

Well, I didn't let it show, but that last comment stung a bit. Oh, I realize that it probably seems odd to someone like Vanessa that my parents are forced to go on furlough every six years to raise support funds. But it's not as if we enjoy this six-month ordeal of tripping about the States begging for money so that my parents can return to the mission field for six more years of hard work and precious little appreciation. Meanwhile, I get stuck in a kids' group home and the mission school. It's not as if we're all over there having a great big party. And it was a low blow for Vanessa to say that about my dad.

But then I guess she can't help it. She takes after her mum. And it was actually her mum's suggestion to take me shopping today. I reckon Aunt Lori's embarrassed to have me seen at their house while my parents are traveling about the States doing "deputation" (which actually means raising mission money). But my dad told me that Aunt Lori was the original "material girl" and that Madonna came up with her song only after meeting her. Of course, he says this with no malice. But it's not exactly a lie either, well, except for the Madonna part, since I'm fairly sure Aunt Lori never actually met the pop star. But certainly no one can deny that Aunt Lori enjoys being rich. I've also heard that my dad's brother, Uncle Ron, never would've gotten this wealthy without his wife's constant "encouragement," which I overheard my mum refer to as "nagging." Mum also said that Lori used to be one of those women with "champagne taste on a beer budget." But it looks like Aunt Lori can have all the champagne she wants now.

To say that I was pretty shocked when I saw how drastically things had changed for my relatives is quite an understatement. The last time we were in the States, back when Vanessa and I were about eleven, they still lived in a regular neighborhood, in a regular sort of three-bedroom house. Oh, her dad's business was doing well and growing, no doubt about that. But they were by no means wealthy, and Vanessa was just a regular girl back then—not all that different from me, other than the accent. But the two of us had such an ace time together, just doing regular things like riding bikes and watching Disney videos and stuff.

But now it seems that everything's changed. Uncle Ron's custodial business has been wildly successful, and as a result it's made their family incredibly wealthy. They now live in this enormous house in a very posh neighborhood and have an inground pool (which I've rather enjoyed this past week), as well as all sorts of other amenities. We're talking lifestyles of the rich and famous here—well, perhaps only *rich*, since Johnson's Janitorial Services may be well known but probably not considered famous, at least not by Hollywood standards. And from what I can see, Hollywood standards seem to rule in my cousin's household—well, at least with Vanessa and Aunt Lori. Uncle Ron still appears to have both feet planted on terra firma.

"Looks like you'll be pretty comfortable this summer, Hannah," my dad observed when we first arrived at their amazing home last week. "Talk about landing in the lap of luxury."

"Are you sure this is the right address?" My mum peered up at the mustard-colored stucco mansion in front of us.

"This is it," said Dad as he pulled our furlough car (an old blue Taurus station wagon with a dent in the right front fender) into the circular driveway, which was lined with pruned shrubs and made entirely of bricks.

"Maybe we shouldn't park our car here," said Mum. "It looks so out of place."

"Do you want me to park it out on the street, Brenda?" My dad's voice was getting slightly irritated now.

Mum laughed nervously. "No, I guess not."

Then Dad reached over and patted her hand. "Don't worry about it, honey. They're still just Ron and Lori, and they still put their pants on one leg at a time."

"But their pants probably cost an arm and a leg now."

As it turned out, Mum was close, because, I kid you not, today I actually witnessed Vanessa purchasing a pair of blue jeans that cost nearly three hundred dollars. Three hundred dollars! I could not believe it. How can a pair of jeans be worth that much?

"Why are they so expensive?" I whispered, not wanting to look like a complete bumpkin as the sales clerk wrapped the precious blue jeans in lavender-colored tissue paper and then slipped them into a sleek bag with ribbon handles.

"They're Armani," she said as if that explained everything. "And besides, they're on sale."

Armani, I said to myself. That must be like Gucci and Prada, the two other designer names I've learned this past week. Now, I can only wonder what that pink plastic Prada purse must've set her back. And I happen to think it's pretty ugly.

So as I sat there in the food court, drinking my lemon squash (known as a Sprite here) and people watching, I began to notice that (a) most of the shoppers were teenage girls or young women, (b) they wore clothes very similar to Vanessa's, (c) they, for the most part, carried bags from the same sorts of stores that Vanessa had been in, and (d) I most definitely did *not* fit in. In fact, I'm sure I looked like something from not only a different country but also an entirely different planet. The funny thing is that all my mates back in PNG dress like this and we were all under the impression that the "grunge look" was still in vogue. But I guess we are behind the times.

It was about then that I noticed this security guard watching me with what I'm sure was suspicion. My guess is that this cop didn't think that I belonged here either and he had probably assumed I was a dodge planning, I'm sure, a great heist. So I just smiled at him and waved. He quickly looked away and then said something into the walkie-talkie thing that was pinned to his chest.

Finally Vanessa came back and, looking over the moon, showed me her prize. "I can't believe I found it," she said as she pulled out a pale blue T-shirt that was so thin you could actually see right through it.

I touched the flimsy fabric. "But won't your bra show through, Vanessa?"

She laughed. "That's the whole point."

"You want the guys to be perving at your bra?"

"I'll make sure to wear a very cool bra with it, Hannah. Don't get all freaked. That's how it's supposed to be."

I tried not to look too stunned, but then I saw the price tag and nearly fell off my chair. "You paid a hundred ninety dollars for *this*?"

She smiled with what I would describe as a condescending

smile (the kind reserved for small children or dimwits) and then gently slipped the shirt back into the bag. "It's a *Prada*—the latest design and the only one left in the store. My friend Elisa is going to be totally jealous."

"Why?"

"Because she wanted one just like it, and now I've gotten the last."

"I'd think your mate would be totally relieved. You just saved her nearly two hundred dollars on a shirt that can't possibly be worth five bucks."

Vanessa laughed. "You just don't get it, Hannah. But wait until you see this top on me, and with my new jeans. Then you might start to understand fashion."

Just then her mobile phone rang, doing its little tinkling musical thing, and suddenly Vanessa was chatting away with one of her mates, going on and on about how she had "searched absolutely everywhere" until she finally found the "perfect Prada T-shirt" and how "hot" she was going to look in it at the party tomorrow night. Yeah, yeah.

I walked over to the bin and dumped my paper cup, pausing to look at that copper who was still eyeing me. Once again, I smiled and waved at him, and to my surprise, he actually smiled back this time. I wanted to walk over and say hello and then ask him what he thought about all these silly girls spending thousands—no make that millions and probably billions—of dollars on strange names like Prada and Gucci and Armani. Did he, like me, think it was perfectly ridiculous? Probably not. After all, this overpriced, designer-driven mall was paying his salary. All right, sometimes I wonder if there's something wrong with me. Why don't I get it? Will I ever really fit in here?

So as I sat there absently listening to Vanessa ear-bashing Elisa

Rodriguez (as it turned out), I started to daydream. I remember this old fairy tale called *The Emperor's New Clothes* that I had enjoyed as a child, only in my mind, I now changed it to the *Empress's New Clothes* (starring Vanessa Johnson). In my version, my cousin insisted that she could only wear the best and most expensive garments in the design industry. "That does not cost enough!" she screams at one of the lesser designers. Finally a designer comes up and says that his outfit will cost one million dollars and will be the most expensive clothing ever made. (Okay, maybe one million dollars is too cheap.) So Empress Vanessa waits for a week, and the designer returns with his "amazing" outfit. But when he opens the gold-plated box with layers of tissue, it is empty. "Where are my clothes?" demands Vanessa. He smiles and says, "Right here, Empress. But you must realize that I have used the finest fibers known to mankind. The threads are so delicate that only those who truly know and appreciate exquisite design can see them." Then, of course, Vanessa nods, pretending she can see the nonexistent clothing. "Go ahead," she tells him. "Help me put them on." And after Vanessa dons her one-million-dollar outfit, she parades all over Beverly Hills in nothing but her underwear, and everyone who sees her simply laughs and—

"Hannah?"

I suddenly look up to see Vanessa standing over me, looking slightly impatient and perhaps a bit weary, although she is fully clothed. "What is it?" I ask sleepily.

"I *said*, are you ready to go home?"

So, the next thing I know, we are driving down the road and, despite all my criticisms of my cousin's lavish lifestyle and expensive taste, I find that I'm enjoying her Yank tank, which is actually this gorgeous silver convertible. It's a Honda S200 and, I reckon, the most luxurious car I've ever been in. I'm leaning back into the soft leather seat as the breeze tosses my hair, and for a brief moment, I imagine what it might feel like to be rich and carefree like my cousin.

But then I look down and notice the hole in the knee of my worn-out cargo pants, and I realize that I am still just Hannah Johnson, the MK misfit from the other side of the world. And all right, I reckon I'm feeling just the slightest bit jealous.